MIDNIGHT, MAGIC, AND NAUGHTY THINGS

MIDNIGHT, MAGIC, AND NAUGHTY THINGS

The moon is full and the night is filled with magic. Join Isabella Jordan for a sensual adventure into the darkness where many decadent delights await you. You'll encounter lusty pirates, magic spells, warlocks, werewolves and dark lovers waiting to steal your heart and make you burn with desire. Experience the night and all of its erotic promises. The darkness awaits…

Previously available only in electronic format, these short stories and novellas have now been combined—due to popular demand—for a paperback edition! Included are...

Electrical Storm
Elegant
Sister Moon
Waiting For You
Woman In Chains

Praise For Isabella Jordan

Elegant

"4.5 Stars...*Elegant* is one of the best short stories I've read all year...Isabella Jordan has created a keeper in that I plan on reading many times in the years to come."

—Nicole Hulst
eCataRomance Reviews

"4 Stars!...A wonderful story!...I'll add this story to my home library and read it over and over again."

—4 stars, Susan Holly
Just Erotic Romance Reviews

Woman In Chains

"Ms. Jordan just keeps getting better and better. You can chain this reviewer up anytime as along as a hero like Anthony is there to save the day."

—Tina Burns
The Road to Romance

"5 Hearts!...Jordan weaves a tale of deceit while justice lies in wait for the truth to appear...Be sure to take time out to read *Woman In Chains*"

—*The Romance Studio*

Electrical Storm

"4 Cups!...Ms. Jordan is a very talented author and one to watch for in the future. If you are looking for a complete and fulfilling, yet compact, story then *Electrical Storm* is the one for you!"

—Susan White
Coffee Time Romance

"...An extremely sexy, erotic, romantic story."

—Ansley Velarde
The Road to Romance

Sister Moon

"4.5 Stars!...I certainly recommend *Sister Moon* to those of you seeking a quick Halloween read with a nice HEA (happily-ever-after) ending and to those of you who, like me, enjoy a good paranormal read."

—Mireya Orsini
Just Erotic Romance Reviews

"4 Hearts!...I recommend this book for lovers of paranormal and especially werewolves."

—Angel Brewer
The Romance Studio

ALSO BY ISABELLA JORDAN

Claiming Michelle
Every Breath You Take
The Legend Of Black Robert Flynne
Stiff Competition

MIDNIGHT, MAGIC, AND NAUGHTY THINGS

BY

ISABELLA JORDAN

AMBER QUILL PRESS, LLC
http://www.amberquill.com

MIDNIGHT, MAGIC, AND NAUGHTY THINGS
AN AMBER QUILL PRESS BOOK

This book is a work of fiction. All names, characters, locations, and incidents are products of the author's imagination, or have been used fictitiously. Any resemblance to actual persons living or dead, locales, or events is entirely coincidental.

Amber Quill Press, LLC
http://www.amberquill.com

ISBN 1-59279-798-9

Layout and Formatting provided by: ElementalAlchemy.com

PUBLISHED IN THE UNITED STATES OF AMERICA

For Jim...

TABLE OF CONTENTS

WAITING FOR YOU

CHAPTER 1

Colleen O'Leary squinted and slowed her car as she passed another street sign. Elyria Avenue. She'd passed that sign three damned times! Where was Harding Avenue? Her new supervisor's birthday party began an hour ago and she had no idea how to get there. Missing the party was a hell of a way to make an impression on Regina Starr who Colleen had yet to meet. The woman had been her boss for less than a week and already Colleen was screwing up.

Well, hell.

The familiar gas station sign—she'd passed it three times, too—was a big fluorescent beacon in the night. Pulling into the gas station parking lot, she sighed in frustration while Bono's soulful tenor sang in the background about streets with no names.

Well, they *did* have names. The wrong damned names!

Blowing a strand of hair off her forehead, Colleen shook her head. She hated having to ask for directions. But she had no choice and no one to blame but herself for the fact she was lost. How hard would it have been to pull up a map on the internet? No, she'd just asked Ned the gardener at the last minute on her way out of her apartment building and had only half listened to what he'd said. And now—

Muttering curses at herself, she parked right in front of the brightly lit store and shut off the engine.

Movements in the shadowy area next to the building caught her eye. Two figures struggled in the dark, one much larger than the other. A woman's black high-heeled shoe skimmed across the pavement into the light and Colleen's heart began to race. What was going on there?

As quietly as she could, she scrambled out of her car, leaving the door ajar. Tiptoeing along the short sidewalk at the front of the building, Colleen crept through the shadows until she reached the edge. Peering around the corner, she saw an enormous man with a woman in his clutches, shaking her.

"Let me go, you bastard!" the woman hissed at him.

The woman, on one high-heel now, struggled to get away from him, though it couldn't have been easy in the tight straight skirt of her business suit. Colleen heard the tearing of fabric as he clutched the back of her jacket and hauled her toward him.

Shit! She had to do *something.*

Colleen flew back to the gas station and raced through the dirty glass door. Her heart pounded as her eyes scanned the small dirty storefront. No one was there!

"Hello!" she shouted.

"I'm in the crapper!" a muffled male voice called from through a door just behind the counter, labeled crudely in black marker CRAPPER.

Colleen flew back out the door and into her car, looking for anything she could use as a weapon. Wildly she fumbled about the car finding an empty soda bottle, the gift bag for her new boss, a paper covered straw. There was an old can of de-icer in the floor at the passenger side. *That might work.* Snatching it up, she jumped back out and headed up the sidewalk, her stride fast and determined.

The man's hands were locked around the woman's throat now and he had her on her knees with her back to Colleen. She tried to get a look at the man, but his face was concealed by the shadows.

The choking sounds coming from the woman spurred Colleen into action.

It's now or never...

With her finger in place on the button of the de-icer can she marched forward and sprayed the man in the face, just as he noticed her approach. The woman was released immediately as he jumped to his feet and attempted to block her chemical attack with his forearm. Colleen turned to see the woman, her long red hair fanning out behind her as she hobbled away as fast as she could on one heel. It was a damned good idea.

Colleen made it all of three feet when the man grabbed her by the hair and pulled her hard against him, her scalp going up in flames of pain in his powerful grip.

"What did you spray me with?" a deep male voice demanded close to her ear. Was that an Irish accent he had?

"De-icer," Colleen bit out. And then remembering she still had the can in her hand, she swung it back towards him as hard as she could. He didn't release her, but the sounds of the metal hitting his face and his surprised grunt were momentarily satisfying.

Colleen strained to see his face in the dark with her peripheral vision as he held there, wiping at his eyes with the sleeve of his jacket. She'd never been so afraid or pissed off in her entire life. The guy had *her* now and unless she caught a break… But at the same time her pride flared at being held there like a dog he'd picked up. *Bastard!*

"You've upset my plans," his accented voice was low, the pronunciation of his words precise.

"Let me go!" Colleen spat.

He released her then and she sure as hell wasn't going to wait for him to change his mind. Colleen tried to speed away. This time he caught her about the waist. Like a cat with a mouse in his large paws, he turned her to face him.

If the devil ever decided on a human form, Colleen was certain he'd choose to look just like the man who held her in the shadows…tall, powerful and handsome with a bold nose, a firm sensual mouth and pale-colored eyes. *He* was pale as far as that was concerned. But the fact that he was remarkably fair took nothing away from the magnificent male specimen she stood gawking at.

Get a grip! The guy could be a serial killer!

Just as Colleen remembered to struggle, she watched his expression change from one of mild interest to…recognition? His eyes rounded in surprise as he stared at her and it stopped Colleen cold. Did she know him from somewhere? She was pretty sure she'd remember someone as striking as he if she'd seen him before.

Something about him was so familiar…

His lips moved, but she couldn't hear what he said for the rushing roar of blood in her ears.

"What?" Colleen whispered.

He pulled her closer, his lips inches from hers. Colleen could smell so many scents on him—the scent of a woman's perfume, the scent of man. Underlying it all was the smell of something dark, sweet, and appealing. The eyes that searched her face were filled with so much emotion she paused.

"Eileen?" he asked.

Only the desperation in his voice kept Colleen from spitting out the sarcastic reply that immediately came to mind. He was looking for something in her eyes, his grip tightened about her waist. Colleen had no choice but to plant her hands on the hard wall of his chest to maintain a distance between them. For all she knew he meant to throttle her as he had the red-haired woman.

Or kiss her.

Either way he's crazy.

"My God, it *is* you," he whispered, lifting a hand to gently catch her jaw.

Colleen shrugged out of his touch and he let her. Her heart was racing and she didn't think that fear was the lone cause of that. The guy thought he *knew* her. This was the same guy she'd watched choke another woman. Well, she didn't want to stick around to find out what happened next even if the guy was sexy as hell. Taking one step backwards, then another, she inched away from him.

"Don't be afraid." His voice was gentle as he moved toward her. "I swear to you that I'd destroy myself before I would ever let any harm come to you."

Destroy himself? What the hell was that supposed to mean?

"That's nice but… a little hard to believe considering you had no trouble strangling that other woman." Colleen swallowed hard, took another step back.

"Eileen, you don't understand—"

"You've got me mixed up with someone else," she cut him off. "That's not my name. I've got to go."

Colleen turned on her heel and sprinted for her car. Just as she reached for the handle of the driver's side door, the door slammed closed and the locks of the car clicked. Her stomach sank as she tried the door handle anyway and discovered she was locked out of her car with her keys still inside.

"Don't be afraid," his voice was a low whisper in her ear.

Colleen jumped in fright to find him standing so close to her. *It was impossible!* He couldn't have moved so quickly. There'd been no footsteps, no movement.

Her eyes locked with his, gray eyes reflecting the harsh light of the store behind her. Holding up a hand before her face like a priest giving a blessing he said, "Sleep and forget."

And Colleen's world went black.

CHAPTER 2

Sean Farrell stared at the woman sleeping in the bed at the center of her dainty bedroom for a long time. The soft light of the lamp on the bedside table reflected off the black silky waves of her hair. Her skin was so white, the features of her face so gentle and perfect. Her lips were full and tender pink and he remembered all too well how sweet they tasted. The soft swell of her breasts beneath the silver blouse she wore trailed off to a tiny waist, slender hips and long, long legs encased in tight black slacks.

He'd never thought to see her again.

Eileen.

It had been two hundred years since Sean had lost her, his wild Irish girl. He'd wanted Eileen Mullins from the moment he first saw her in the village they were from, selling vegetables from her father's farm for money. The poor country girl with her bouncy black curls and torn dirty dress was a far cry from the sleek woman sprawled across the bed before him. But it *was* her. The fiery green eyes were exactly the same, her spirit…

Pain Sean thought long vanquished rose to the surface with frightening ease. Eileen's father had died the eve of her eighteenth birthday. Sean had planned to marry Eileen, to save the farm for her and make right in the Almighty's eyes what they did when they were alone. Sean could still remember the day Eileen had first given herself to him in her father's barn, the wildflowers he'd picked for her tucked recklessly in her hair. He could feel the tight buds of her nipples between his lips as if he'd tasted them yesterday. The memory of her tight little pussy closing around him as he drove inside her had him hard and ready now, making him long to join her on that bed and make love to her for days.

She'd loved him. Called him her Sean...

And then evil had taken her away from him in the form of a devious creature, Regan Sheehan he'd known her as, who preyed on the women of Eileen's bloodline. How damned ironic was it that the very night he finally caught the bitch, the one who'd murdered Eileen all those years before, he found Eileen too? His love born again in this century…

His hunger for the woman on the bed before him explained everything he'd done. When he'd lost her, he'd lost himself. Sean had sold himself to the darkness, stalked and begged the vampire who had become his maker for the chance to have his revenge against the monster who'd destroyed Eileen through immortality. For decades he tracked Regan Sheehan knowing that even if he succeeded, it was a hollow victory. After that, what did he have but an eternity to suffer the endless night alone as a vampire?

But Eileen had come back to him.

Colleen, he reminded himself. That was the name on her driver's license anyway.

There'd been no recognition at all in her eyes, but he'd cultivate the memories slowly over time. Sean relished the thought of helping Colleen to remember him, of creating new memories with her in bed and out. She was his forever now. He'd never let her go.

For the first time in centuries Sean knew happiness.

She *would* love him again, Sean vowed. No matter how long it took, no matter what he had to do, he'd have her heart again. He'd have her in his bed and every way imaginable. And this time they would enjoy the pleasures they'd only begun to explore when they were young and in love so many years ago in Ireland.

Oh, there was so much he longed to do with her. *To* her. His cock ached just thinking about it.

But tonight was a bad way to start, Sean decided as his gaze swept around her bedroom. In his defense, finding her again was the last thing he would ever have expected. It was bad luck that she had to find him trying to kill Regan Sheehan, whom he'd finally caught up with after so many years.

But being a vampire had its uses. Sean had used his dark gifts to wipe her mind clean of the incident at the gas station and put her into a deep sleep. He'd gently loaded Colleen into her car, found the driver's license in her purse for an address, and brought her home. She'd awaken in the morning wondering what the hell happened the evening before, safe in her bed, yet unsure.

And then they would begin again. Sean grinned in anticipation.

Rising from the chair by her bed, his gaze fastened on the desk in the cluttered corner of the room. The rest of her apartment was neat as a pin compared to that corner with its boxes of files, zip disks, and CDs nestled around a desk that held a computer and an assortment of cameras, scanners, printers. All of it state-of-the-art.

More than that were personal touches. A little pair of reading glasses rested atop a scanner and a box of tissues next to the printer. An empty glass sat before the monitor of her computer.

She spends a lot of time here.

It would be so much easier for Sean to seduce her if she were a social butterfly, but Colleen was apparently an introvert in this life. A computer geek no less.

No matter. Seduce her he would. It was the quickest way to achieve his goals of reclaiming her for himself and keeping her safe from Regan Sheehan because there was one thing he was fairly certain of…

Colleen was the intended victim of Regan Sheehan. *Again.*

Sean had been tracking Regan for weeks now and he'd watched her behavior grow more and more erratic. She planned to claim her next victim soon, he just knew it. It took a predator to know one. The fact that Eileen—*Colleen*—just happened to be in the same area was too coincidental. It *had* to be Colleen she was hunting.

To protect Colleen Sean would need to know as much as he could about her. Pulling out the chair at her desk, he sat down and turned on her computer.

CHAPTER 3

Colleen slumped in her chair in the noisy nightclub of the conference hotel and shook her head at the melee all around her. Now she remembered why she'd sworn off computer conferences. *God Almighty.* There were guys in horned rimmed glasses and pocket protectors in their shirt pockets up for karaoke with flowerpots on their heads singing Devo's *Whip It.* Another group of nerdy computer experts crowded the tables closest to the stage cheering them with loud yells and whistles.

The salespeople haunted the back of the room as she did. They were younger men and women, mostly one to a table, wearing immaculate suits and talking on cell phones or pecking away at the keyboards of their laptops. The expressions they wore told Colleen they were tired or stressed. Or just plain bored.

Finished with their song, the nerds onstage pulled off their flowerpots and started doing the robot for their next song. It had been ten years since she'd heard the song *Mr. Roboto.* Their singing was so bad she hoped it was ten more years before she heard it again.

"May I join you?"

The seductive voice close to her ear gave her a start.

Colleen glanced up into the most beautiful, crystal clear gray eyes she'd ever seen. *And the rest of him is mighty fine too.* A tall, gorgeous man with thick blonde hair that just reached his collar, and shoulders wide as the bedroom door stood by the table waiting for her reply.

Well, don't just stare at him. Say something!

Colleen nodded. "Sure."

He smiled at her then. And Colleen thought he was gorgeous before? His smile was a flash of white that had her insides humming. His face was perfect, all hard angles that softened just enough when he smiled. Colleen squirmed in her seat as he pulled out the chair next to hers and sat down.

"So how did you get roped into this?" he asked.

Oh, an Irish accent. Colleen watched him place his elbows on the table before him and lean toward her. He smelled wonderful, light spicy cologne blended with the smell of man. A corner of his mouth lifted into a cocky half-smile, but his eyes were intent on her, his gaze moving over her hair and face. His close proximity had tingles of excitement racing through her body.

"Well?" he prompted, his smile widening at her hesitation.

Oh, shit. What was the question?

"My company sent an email this morning," she remembered, "telling me that they wanted me to come to this at the last minute. I have a new supervisor and from what I hear she is sending everyone to conferences or seminars for new ideas and to promote the company. It would have been nice to have a little more warning."

"From what you *hear* of your new supervisor?" his tone had a hint of teasing. "Don't you ever go in to work?"

Colleen shook her head. "I telecommute. I haven't even met my new supervisor yet."

And that reminded her of the birthday party her company had held for her new boss the night before. Colleen had *planned* to go. She'd even gotten in the car intending to go and…well, she didn't know what had happened then. She'd awakened at home in her bed, still dressed and found the birthday present meant for her new boss on her kitchen table. It didn't make any sense and it had been on her mind ever since. For all she knew sending her to this conference was her new boss' way of getting back at her for missing the party. She didn't *mean* to miss it, had no idea what happened.

"What are you thinking about?" Her companion's deep voice broke into her thoughts.

Colleen shook her head, not about discuss last night's events with him. "Nothing."

"Well, something caused you to lose your happy thoughts," he pointed out.

"It's okay," Colleen waved it away. Besides, she had something else to deal with just now—the handsome stranger sitting next to her. Colleen had seen very few men in her entire life that looked *that* good. And he was sitting with *her*. Okay, so she didn't get out much. But damn, it was exciting. Especially considering the fact that she hadn't been in any sort of relationship—or had sex—in almost a year. Idly she wondered how big a piece he was packing.

Okay, it's been way too long since you got laid, Colleen.

"Why are *you* here?" Colleen steered the conversation away from herself, away from dirty thoughts.

"I work for a home security systems company," he explained. "Computer-human interaction plays an important part in my business. Seemed a worthwhile conference to attend."

"Has it been worthwhile?" Colleen didn't think so. As far as the conference was concerned anyway.

"It's definitely getting better." His smiled widened as he held out his hand. "I'm Sean Farrell."

"Colleen O'Leary." She took his hand expecting him to shake it. Instead he turned her wrist so he could kiss the back of her hand in an old-fashioned way. The warm press of his lips to her skin sent pleasurable waves coursing through her body and her nipples beaded hard.

"So what do you want from me, handsome?" Colleen decided to cut to the chase. Was he hitting on her? Trying to sell her something?

Sean's gray eyes darkened, looked stormy. He didn't release her hand but captured it between his two larger ones. "I want *you*."

Well, hell, isn't that the direct approach? A hundred reactions raced through her head as she stared mutely at him, trying to recover.

"If you are going to ask questions, be prepared for the answers." Sean's voice was low. His eyes searched hers, his expression stilled and serious. He wasn't playing with her. Sean still held her hand between his; the pad of one of his thumbs delicately traced a line back and forth across the sensitive flesh of her wrist. She felt his touch all over her body and the flesh between her thighs began to soften and warm.

What if he's a psycho?

But her body wasn't buying that. She wasn't pulling her hand away, was she? Was it the fact that she hadn't had sex for a long time that had her gawking at him like a schoolgirl? Or was it the fact that he looked better than any man she could conjure in her wildest sexual fantasies?

"Does that line usually work?" Colleen finally spoke, her words meant to back him off. But to her frustration her voice was shaky and he appeared unmoved.

"Line? No." Sean's gaze never wavered. "Once you know me better you'll know I never speak lightly."

Colleen's heart beat wildly and she swallowed hard. Sean's eyes darted to the movement of her throat and quickly back. *This guy could be a rapist, a killer.* But honestly she knew her heart was racing as much from excitement as it was from fear. The most sinfully handsome man she'd ever met had just told her in a very direct way that he wanted her. *My, my, my...*

"And who says that I *will* get to know you better?" Colleen had to ask.

"I do."

His fingers pushed under the sleeve of her blouse, began smoothing over the skin of her inner forearm. Colleen's breath caught at her body's reaction, at the craving that built in her pussy from just that simple touch. What she wouldn't have given to be able to slide her hand into her panties, stroke herself… Or better yet to feel his fingers slide into her folds.

There was a confidence in Sean's smile, like the handsome devil could read her mind or something. His knee brushed hers under the table and she jumped. How good it would have felt to capture that powerful leg between hers, to rub herself against…

Colleen, what's gotten into you?

Colleen shook her head to clear it. She was drowning in his eyes and all caught up in a lust like nothing she'd ever experienced. She had to stop this now if she was going to. Yanking her arm away from him, she jumped up from the chair.

"Look, I don't do this sort of thing." Maybe she wanted to, but she didn't. Colleen tore her gaze away from his as she grabbed her jacket from the back of the chair, snatched up her briefcase from the floor.

"Good," he said simply.

That got her attention. Stopping in her tracks she met his gaze squarely. "What?"

"I'm glad you don't *do* this sort of thing." His hand reached for her, but she stepped back to avoid his touch. If he touched her again, she was afraid she might drag him back to her room and jump his bones. The effect he had on her was *that* strong. "I don't want you to know another man's touch. I am going to be the last lover you'll ever have, Colleen."

Colleen sped away from the table at that. The wet cotton of her panties rubbed against her as she walked quickly down the hallway towards the elevator. Nervous excitement still coursed through her as she stepped out of the crowded elevator on the fourth floor and she couldn't get his words out her head.

I am going to be the last lover you'll ever have, Colleen.

He might have been suggesting that he would kill her. The only other thing it could have meant is that he planned to be with her for her the rest of her life and…

That's ridiculous! No, not going to analyze this. Put it out of your head.

Colleen's hand shook as she fished the card to her hotel room out of her jacket pocket, making her struggle to fit into the slot of her hotel room. She cried out when a larger hand closed over hers and steadied it so the card could slide into the slot.

Now she *was* afraid as she slowly turned around to face Sean, who towered over her and pinned her to the spot with those stormy gray eyes. If he'd sped up there to catch her before she'd entered her room, it didn't show. He was perfectly calm, perfectly composed as his eyes searched hers. *Hell, he's not even breathing hard.*

"What do you want?" Colleen's voice was a hoarse whisper.

"I think we've already covered that." Sean made no move to touch her, stood almost *too* still in the hallway gazing down at her.

"Do you mean to hurt me?" Colleen looked up and down the hallway, hoping someone else would happen by. But surely there were people in the rooms on her floor. "I'll scream."

"I would never hurt you, Colleen," his expression softened just a little. "And I won't allow anyone else to. *Ever*. I promise you that."

Colleen's mind was spinning even as her body resumed its ache. Every nerve ending in her body was electrified and the craving in her hot, wet center grew. God help her, she wanted him, this stranger who showed up out of nowhere. But the things he said… It was insane. He didn't know her. How could he say—

"And I *want* you to scream," Sean's seductive voice broke into her thoughts. "But I want you to scream in pleasure for me. I want you to scream with my cock inside you, bringing you unimaginable pleasure again and again for as long as you can take it."

Colleen released the breath she hadn't realized she'd been holding. His coat was open enough for her to see the sizeable bulge encased in the denim of his jeans and her pussy ached. Her body needed him inside her, instinctively knowing that a night with him would be unlike anything she'd ever known in her thirty-one years.

But she couldn't just fuck a stranger! Could she? Not that anyone would know, but still…

Her hand fumbled behind her for the doorknob to her room and found it.

What's it going to be, Colleen?

Colleen took a deep breath before saying, "I can't."

Again, he seemed unmoved. "Why?" he asked, his voice a seductive purr. "Are you married? Are you seeing someone, Colleen?"

I love the way he says my name with that accent.

Her voice sounded small. "No."

"Then you can do anything you wish," Sean continued. "You can cry out for help or walk into your room alone. I won't stop you."

Yes, she could and *should* do one or both of those things.

"Or you can give in to what your body wants." Gently he lifted a lock of hair from her shoulder, rubbing the strands between his fingers and thumb. "I will fulfill every desire you've ever had, Colleen. I promise you won't regret it."

I'll just bet I wouldn't.

Colleen turned the knob of the door and pushed it open. All she had to do was back into the room and close the door. That's all she had to do.

She took a step back and then another. Standing just inside the doorway of her room, she watched for his reaction. But he only waited silently, unmoving. The hunger in his eyes was unmistakable.

Well, if he was so bound and determined to have her, why did he just stand there?

"I can't enter unless you invite me in," Sean explained as if in answer to her thought.

It's now or never. Make the call.

"Come in," Colleen whispered.

CHAPTER 4

Sean struggled for control as he closed the door behind them and locked it. His hunger for the taste of her blood, the need to have his cock inside her *now* were damned near overwhelming. It had been easy to tell her that he'd allow her to call for help or walk into her hotel room alone, but he wasn't at all sure he would have allowed her to had she not invited him in.

But she *had* invited him in. Sean knew triumph as he watched her set her briefcase on the table by the window and drape her jacket across it with her little hands trembling. While Sean could feel her fear of him, he could also smell the delicate aroma of her excitement. Desire had control of her at the moment and he meant to keep it that way. Especially considering what she would learn this night.

"This is crazy," she said, eyeing him warily from where she stood by the bed.

God, he'd forgotten how beautiful she was. Sean closed the distance between them to take her in his arms and he wanted to howl with joy at being able to hold her again. It took every ounce of restraint he had not to crush her against him, but crush her he could. She was mortal, his Colleen, as he had not been for a very long time. It was a fact Sean couldn't allow himself to forget because it would be so easy for him to hurt her if he were the least bit careless.

"What is crazy about it, Colleen?" Sean bent low to brush his lips to the white flesh of her throat. Fresh blood rushed through her veins, her heartbeat a relentless staccato in his ears. "I want you and I mean to have you."

Her emerald green eyes flashed up at him, filled with desire and hesitation. Anything but desire would soon be eradicated, he promised himself. Sean didn't give a damn who feared him, and most creatures that walked the earth had reason to fear him, but not his love.

"You want me, too, or you wouldn't have invited me to your bed." Sean worked the buttons of her blouse, captured her lips for a kiss. *Ah, God, it was her.* Her sweet taste was manna to his senses after so many years. He deepened the kiss, coaxing her lips apart. Colleen's slight form trembled in his arms, but she returned his kiss, allowed him to pull off her blouse and her bra and wrapped her arms around his neck, her hands sliding up into his hair. Sean closed his eyes, reveling in her exquisite touch.

Sean cupped her ass in his hands and lifted her easily from the floor. He lowered her onto the bed, snatching off the dark slacks she wore before she even knew what happened. His coat and shirt were tossed away with the same preternatural speed. He grinned at the disorientation in her eyes. His movements had been too fast for her mortal eyes. He lowered his body onto her, spread her beneath him.

Sean took one of her nipples greedily into his mouth as he slid a hand down her belly and into her panties. Her pussy was hot and ready, slick with her need for him. Oh yes, he'd fulfill her needs and desires just as he'd promised. Colleen clung to him in her passion, her desire for him was intoxicating. The night stretched out before them and Sean planned to be inside of her for most of it. He wanted to feel her wrapped around his cock, see how much she could take, how many times she could take it.

Colleen squirmed beneath him, her long supple legs wrapping about his thighs as he slid first one finger and then another into her wet passage.

"Do you like that, Colleen?" Sean loved the way her head tossed back and forth on the bed, insane from his touch. "Or do you want more? Would you like my mouth on you?"

"Yes!" Her little hands clutched at his shoulders, his hair.

Sean slid down her body, remembering too well how much she loved his mouth between her legs. Her thighs parted like water under his hands, making it easy for him to rip off her panties and dive for her with his mouth. The smell of her intimate treasure had him burning, heightening his lust tenfold. His lips and tongue worked into the sable curls at the top of her thighs, finding the slick inner flesh weeping for his touch. Colleen went wild above him, grabbing his hair, thrusting herself at his mouth. Sean gave her all she wanted, teasing the hard little nub of her clit with his tongue, tasting the walls of her passage with quick, stiff thrusts. Sean kept at her relentlessly until she climaxed, her nectar sweet on his tongue as she rode his mouth in abandon.

Sean couldn't wait any longer. He'd removed the last of his clothing while the last of the tremors shook her. Lowering his body onto hers, Sean entered her with a single, smooth thrust, loving the way her flesh stretched and gave to make room until she'd taken every inch of him. Colleen wrapped herself around him, pulled his head down for a kiss and he took her lips greedily while his cock began a steady determined rhythm within her. Her pussy was so tight around him, clinging to him with each thrust. It was hell to have to restrain himself, to not be able to ride her with abandon, but he managed. His Colleen was fragile, no match for his strength at all. But she felt so damned good as he pulled out of her and slid back in.

"Harder," Colleen gasped into his mouth. "I want it harder!"

Knowing she was close to coming, Sean increased the power of his thrusts as much as he dared. It didn't take much. Colleen cried out, her nails digging into his back as he drove on, her body quivering sweetly around him as she found her release.

But Sean wasn't ready yet to give into release himself. He took possession of her again, teasing her with slow, steady thrusts until her belly tightened and the tension in her limbs returned. Sean started pumping her harder, faster to bring her to climax again.

"Shall I stop now, Colleen?" Sean whispered in her ear before dipping his head to kiss the sweet flesh of her neck, the pulsing of the warm vein beneath the skin beckoning him as he continued to move his cock in and out of her.

"No, please!"

"Then come again for me." Sean licked that vein, he couldn't help it. "Cover me with your honey again."

And oh, she did. Sean took her cries into his mouth as she tightened around him, her hands desperate on his back. He pushed into her faster, heightening her climax as he allowed himself release. Sean felt as if he'd exploded as he pumped his seed into her, bursting into thousands of tiny microscopic pieces. It was so damned good, beyond anything he'd ever experienced or remembered.

Collapsing onto the bed beside her, Sean stretched out on his back, pulling her against him. He'd be ready to go again any time, but he had to admit he enjoyed the way Colleen snuggled against him, her head resting on his chest. Her hair was a glossy black river flowing over his shoulder and arm. All around them was the smell of sex, her secret smell. Sean closed his eyes, overjoyed that she was his, in his arms.

Colleen surprised him out of his contented lull by jerking her head up from his chest, her eyes round with fear as they locked with his.

"I can't h-hear your heart," her breath was coming fast.

Sean knew he shouldn't be eyeing the full white globes of her breasts just then, but for a moment he couldn't help it, their movement was so enticing.

"Did you hear me?" she persisted, pressing her hands to his chest now, and he met her gaze. "I can't feel your heart beating."

Well, they were going to have to talk about it sooner or later.

"My heart stopped beating a long time ago, Colleen," Sean said calmly.

Colleen's face turned white, her beautiful green eyes filled with fear. Sean could almost feel the adrenaline rushing through her body and she looked ready to flee at any second. Not that it would do her a lot of good. No way in hell he was letting her go anywhere without him. Ever.

"Let's talk," he said.

CHAPTER 5

Colleen stared at Sean, her heart hammering in her chest. The sexiest man she'd ever seen had just given her the fuck of her life. Her insides were still pulsing and her legs felt so wobbly she would have been amazed if they could hold her up. But she should have listened to her gut that something was wrong with the whole situation, should have known there was something wrong with *him.*

And she'd just had unprotected sex with him. Shit!

"We don't have to talk." Colleen edged away from him on the bed. "You don't have to tell me anything. We've had our fun and I think you should go now."

She made it to the edge of the bed and he made no move to stop her. So far, so good. Still it was unnerving the way he lay there staring at her, not moving, not blinking.

Colleen snatched her clothes up from the floor.

"I'm going to go to the lobby for a soda," Colleen tried to sound calm, but she failed miserably. "When I get back I expect you to be gone."

But she could put her clothes on later. All she really needed at the moment in her panic was her coat. It was long enough to cover her until she could get to a restroom to get dressed anyway. Clutching her clothes to her breasts, she backed away towards the door. Just a few more steps and she'd have her coat…

Colleen spun around to snatch the coat from the peg by the hotel door, began to frantically pull it on.

"Neither one of us is leaving, Colleen," his voice was a silken purr in her ear.

Colleen jumped and screamed to find him standing behind her at the door. *No way!* But there he stood in all his naked glory, his erection hard and ready as he forced her back a step.

Sean had no heartbeat and he could disappear and reappear whenever he wished. And they were both naked and he was stalking her, backing her in the direction of the bed. Roughly he grabbed the clothes and coat from her hands and hurled them to the floor.

"Who are you?" she whispered, her hands rising to cover her breasts. "*What* are you?"

Colleen had never been so afraid or turned on in her life. Her gaze dropped to his erection and she swallowed hard, her thighs still trembling from his loving. She'd give almost anything for him to take her again, to have him driving inside her just like he had moments ago.

But what the hell was going on? Because there was something not right about him.

"Colleen," his deep voice was the only sound in the dark room as her gaze locked with his. "Remember that I promised I would never hurt you? I meant that. Don't be afraid of me."

"What *are* you?" Colleen demanded as he clutched her upper arms in hands. The sheer strength of him made her quiver. So much leashed power in his muscular body. "How can you just move around like that? You scared the shit out of me!"

Sean smiled, such a beautiful self-assured smile. "Don't fear me. I'll tell you everything."

He pushed her back down on the bed, hauling her up the mattress until her feet no longer hung off the edge. His weight settled over hers, his knees wedging between hers and pushing her legs apart. The hot shaft of his cock twitched against her inner thigh.

And she wanted that cock inside her again. Badly.

"Colleen, look at me."

She gazed up into his eyes and the intensity in them nearly took her breath away.

"I was once mortal like you, an ordinary man," Sean spoke slowly. "But that mortal life is long gone from this body."

"Mortal?" Colleen's mind scrambled. Was he crazy then? Was that it? Was he going to tell her he was an alien or something? "You mean human?"

"Yes." Sean's cock moved up to tease the outer lips of her pussy. "I mean human. I haven't been human for a very long time."

Colleen shook her head. *Great! He's a nut job.*

"No, I'm a vampire."

"What?"

Colleen watched in stunned silence as his eyes glowed silver, pure silver light in the darkness above her. There was just enough light from the window by the bed for her to see the white flash of his teeth as he bared them. While she watched, his incisors grew, long and sharp.

Oh, shit!

Collaring her wrists in his hands, Sean held her to the bed while she struggled.

A vampire! Vampires weren't supposed to be real! They were characters in movies, in books by drunk and demented Irishmen. They weren't supposed to be walking around in society, materializing around people. In their beds…

Sean's cock slid into her folds, poised at her aching opening. Incredible as scared as she was of the man—vampire—who pinned her to the bed that she still had any thoughts of having sex with him again.

Oh, but she did. God help her, she did.

"Vampires aren't real," she said, more for herself than him. *But how did you explain the glowing? The fangs? The fact that he could materialize wherever he wanted to?* But as Colleen watched, his eyes stopped glowing, his fangs retracted. *How else could you explain it?* "Oh, my God."

Sean dipped his head to brush her lips with a tender kiss. "I would never hurt you, Colleen."

"You're going to drink my blood then?" It wasn't lost on her just how corny that question sounded.

"I need to taste your blood, yes." His voice was low, rough with desire. "But for selfish reasons. I'd never feed on you. You're too precious to me."

Colleen frowned at him. "You don't even know me."

Sean's cock slid into her at that moment, a slow push until he filled her completely and Colleen gasped. *He feels so good.* He began a slow, luxurious rhythm within her and she was more than ready and willing, vampire or not. Wrapping her legs around his waist, she tried to hurry him, to urge him to go faster. His grip on her wrists tightened as he pushed her thighs wider apart, deepening his penetration.

Colleen moaned, the pleasure unreal. Whatever the hell he was, she loved the way his cock stuffed her, the way he totally dominated her.

"I'll give you what you want," he whispered, teasing her lower lip with his own as he slid in and out of her pussy with a maddeningly slow cadence. "If you'll give me what I want."

When his lips slid down to tease her nipple, Colleen gasped, pushing herself up into his mouth, lost in the incredible pleasure of his lovemaking. She'd give him anything if he'd just keep fucking her this way. Anything…

"But what do you want? I've already given you—"

Sean cut her off. His lips reclaimed hers in a slow, enticing kiss. When he finally lifted his head, she managed to ask, "My blood?"

His thrusts grew in strength and she raised her hips to meet each one, never wanting his loving to end. She was so close to release, so close…

"Your trust," Sean said finally, gazing deeply into her eyes as he released her wrists. Colleen wrapped her arms around his neck, pulled his mouth down to hers for another kiss, another taste of him. His pace within her quickened, bringing her so close to release. Colleen held onto to him, bracing for the climax, wanting it. But just as she was about to have it he slowed and she cried out in frustration.

"Patience, my love," he whispered, his lips burning a trail across her cheek to her neck. "First I would have your promise."

His lips teased her neck while his cock teased her with its slow drag and push. Colleen froze, her heart hammered in her chest. Sean was poised at her jugular. *Oh, God.*

"Promise me your trust, Colleen," Sean whispered against her skin. "All I want is to taste you."

But he was going to bite her neck with those sharp teeth. Colleen didn't like needles and she was sure she wouldn't like him biting her.

But she really wanted to come again and she just knew he'd withhold that treat from her until she relented. *Damn him!*

"Just a taste?" Colleen was hesitant.

His cock thrust powerfully inside her and again. *That's it. I want that. Make it hard.*

"Just a taste," he whispered.

When his delicious movements inside her slowed again, she cried out in frustration.

"Okay!" she promised, frustrated.

Sean chuckled against her throat, a deep rich sound.

Colleen winced as she felt him nick her throat with his teeth.

Sean's body began to thrust harder into hers, faster. *Yes, that's it.*

His cock was so good, stuffed her completely. Colleen came almost immediately after that, her arms and legs wrapped around the hard, muscular length of his body as she cried out in pleasure. It really didn't hurt so bad when his fangs slid into her neck and after… His hands cupped her ass, angling her so that he could penetrate her from just the right angle. He withdrew only slightly before pushing back into her. He did that several times, teasing and exciting her until she felt ready to explode. Sean made her come again and again, while Colleen thrashed wildly beneath him, a slave to the passion he'd ignited in her.

She didn't know how much time had passed when he finally lifted his head from her throat, threw it back as he allowed himself release, his arms tightening around her until it almost hurt.

Colleen felt lightheaded when Sean collapsed on top of her. From the power of his loving? From blood loss? Who knew? And she didn't give a good damn in that moment with his delicious weight on her and the soothing feeling of his hands in her hair.

But as exhausted as she was, she couldn't shut off her mind.

"Sean?"

"Hmm?"

"You're really a vampire."

"I really am."

"What did you mean when you said you would be the last lover I ever had?" Colleen wanted to know. "If you don't mean to kill me… What did you mean by that?"

Sean rolled off of her, much to her disappointment, but pulled her body against his so that he spooned up behind her. The feeling of his hard thighs behind her quivering ones was nice. *Very nice.*

"I meant just what I said, Colleen." His voice just behind her ear made her shiver. "No other man will ever touch you. You're mine. You've always been mine."

Sean's hand slid down from her waist to capture her hand, his fingers interlacing with hers.

"But how do you know me?" Colleen knew she'd never seen him before tonight. "How have I always been yours?"

"Sleep now, my love," was all he said. "You need your rest now."

"You promised to tell me everything," Colleen reminded him.

"I will." Sean pressed a kiss into her hair. "Sleep now."

And even though she'd just had the most amazing sex of her entire life twice *and* learned that her lover was a vampire of all damned things, she drifted off to sleep.

CHAPTER 6

Colleen shot up in bed in fear, soaked with sweat, her heart pounding. Sleep still clouded her mind so when her eyes adjusted to the darkness and she didn't find the comforting familiarity of her bedroom, her panic escalated. Someone had been stalking her in her nightmare, a woman with long red hair whose face transformed... *Oh, how horrible it had been.* Though Colleen had awakened from the dream before the woman managed to catch her, she instinctively knew the woman meant her harm.

Sean sat up in bed next to her, cradled her in his arms and Colleen curled into him. He'd been in her dream too. At least he'd tried to help her.

"What did you dream about?" Sean's voice was gentle.

"A woman who was trying to kill me," Colleen explained, her voice scratchy from sleep. "She had long red hair and a horrible face. She started out pretty, but her face changed, like it aged very fast. God, it seemed so real."

Sean's hands smoothed her hair, caressed her back. "She can't hurt you, Colleen. I'm here."

Colleen smiled against his chest, liking the way he comforted her. "I know. It was just a dream."

"What else do you remember about the dream?" he asked, reaching behind her to snap on the lamp of the bedside table.

"Why do you want to know?" It took a moment for Colleen's eyes to adjust to the light. Her gaze immediately found Sean and her heart quickened. He was impossibly gorgeous with his rumpled blonde hair, the smooth, hairless planes of his chest all powerful muscles.

Sean pulled her back into his arms, gazing down into her eyes. "Tell me."

Dreams fell away so fast after one awakened, but Colleen remembered a few things. "We were in the country, on a farm. One reason I thought she'd catch me is that I was wearing this ridiculous long dress, old-fashioned you know. And I remember she trapped me in an old barn. You were outside the doors, but you couldn't get in and then her face changed and looked so gross."

Sean's face was a mask of implacable calm, but she could sense emotion just beneath the surface. Why was he taking her dream so seriously?

"Then I woke up," Colleen explained. "Just in time."

Sean's arms tightened around her and he lifted a hand to her face, his fingertips lightly tracing the line of her jaw. "Colleen, I've something to tell you and it may be hard for you to accept at first."

Colleen snorted. "And you telling me that you are a vampire *wasn't*?" She was still processing that one. "By all means, tell me."

Sean's gray eyes searched hers. "That wasn't a dream, Colleen, but a memory of something that actually happened a long time ago."

There'd been a quality about the beginning of the dream that *had* seemed very real, like it might have happened. But then the woman had cornered her in the barn and she transformed into something hideous.

No, monsters didn't exist. That part of the dream was just like all of the other nonsensical episodes in her head at night that she sometimes remembered.

But vampires exist.

No *way* that scene in her dream really happened. *No way!*

"But it did," Sean said aloud. And it wasn't the first time he'd responded aloud to her thoughts.

Turning on Sean, Colleen caught him off guard and shoved him away from her. Or, closer to the truth, he *let* her.

"You can read my mind, can't you?" Colleen snapped.

At least he had the decency to look a little guilty. "Yes."

"Well, stop it! My thoughts are none of your business!"

Sean propped a pillow against the headboard behind him and leaned back against it, making himself comfortable. Was this all a game to him? *Damn him!*

"I can't avoid it really," Sean explained. "When I was first made, all the voices in the heads of others were deafening, drove me mad. Now, they are quiet, whispers in my mind, but I still hear them whether I want to or not."

"Well, ignore mine because they are *none* of your business," Colleen wanted him to know.

"I'll remember that," Sean assured her, a corner of his mouth lifting into half-grin.

"And my reality has been stretched as far as it is going to stretch, okay?" Colleen looked him in the eye, thinking that the reality wasn't the only thing that had been stretched to its limits as she hopped off the bed, sore in places she couldn't name. She hated to pace, but he'd driven her to it. Back and forth she paced by the bed and she didn't even give a damn that she was naked. What was the point of getting dressed? He'd seen everything she had and he could probably see through her clothes anyway.

"Last night I headed out for a birthday party for my new boss," Colleen began, "which I apparently never made it to because I woke up *in* my house, *in* my clothes with her birthday present on the kitchen table. *Then* I get an email from work sending me to BoringCon 2004 at the last minute, but that got a lot more interesting when *you* showed up, didn't it? I just jumped in bed with you—which I never do by the way. And guess what? You're a *vampire* of all damned things. And then I have a dream—"

"Colleen, it's okay," Sean whispered as his arms closed around her, making her jump in fright. Her gaze shot to the bed where he'd just been reclining and found it empty—foolish she knew since there he was holding her to his chest and soothing her like a frightened child.

Screw that!

"Stop doing that!" Colleen pushed away from him.

"I'm sorry," Sean's tone was calm. "I know you're upset."

"Damn right I'm upset." Tears stung the back of her eyes. "How do you expect me to feel? You're a vampire for God's sake!"

When he took a step towards her, she held up a hand to ward him off, and let the tears come. Colleen was afraid; she was pissed off. She wanted him to stay the hell away from her; she wanted him to hold her.

"Colleen, you dreamed of something that happened over two hundred years ago in Ireland. You lived with your father on a farm and I was in love with you."

She swiped angrily at her tears with the back of her hand as he approached, but she let him walk up behind her and wrap his arms around her. At least he didn't just *appear* behind her.

"Two hundred years ago?" Colleen couldn't keep the skepticism from her voice.

"Yes." Sean kissed the top of her head. "Your father died when you were just eighteen years old. Liam was his name and he was a good man. There was no truer man to his word than Liam Mullins."

The name meant nothing to Colleen. It didn't even sound familiar.

"I planned to marry you if you'd have me," he went on, his voice full of emotion. "I had no money for a ring, but I picked some of your favorite flowers—the purple ones that grew in the field by the river at the edge of your farm."

Colleen hooked her hands around his arms, hanging on. For what, she didn't know yet. His words were sweet, but sparked no memory. Purple was her favorite color, that was about it.

"Regan Sheehan had once been a midwife in the village," Sean continued. "But when the babes she birthed started to die, the people ran her out of town, accused her of being a witch. Your father never believed what everyone said about her and I guess I always thought she had set her cap for him. I had no idea it was you she was after."

Still, nothing rang a bell. But she was curious.

"Regan Sheehan, huh? And she was after *me?*"

"The woman with the red hair from your dream... She murdered you."

Colleen felt a shudder go through his body as his arms tightened about her. "It happened so damned fast. I wanted to tear down the door to that barn, to tear her limb from limb. But when I finally broke in there..."

When his voice faltered, she turned in his arms to face him. The raw emotion on his handsome face moved her to pity as he continued.

"She's a monster," he explained. "She steals the bodies of women within her bloodline. *Your* bloodline."

Colleen frowned. "Steals bodies?"

Sean's eyes glowed briefly as they locked with hers, his hands catching her upper arms so quickly she flinched. But his grip didn't hurt. Somehow she knew he'd never hurt her.

"I've followed her for decades now. Whatever she is, she can't inhabit the same body for more than fifteen, twenty years. That or it is youth she's after. When her current body starts to age, she discards it for a younger one."

Colleen's heart raced in her chest. "She stole *my* body? Is that what you are saying? In a former life she stole my body?"

Maybe he was crazy after all.

"Yes, she did." A muscle in Sean's jaw twitched as he spoke, gripped by the memory he shared with her. "She stood there in your body, smiling at me. And I didn't understand what happened at the time. I didn't know that the rotting shell she left laying on the ground was the body she'd left behind. But I *knew* that it wasn't *you,* your soul, gazing out at me through those beautiful green eyes."

Colleen was sure of one thing. He believed everything he told her. The conviction in his eyes and voice spoke volumes. She felt her disbelief start to crack. Could there be any truth to what he'd said?

"But you're *here* now. You came back to me." Sean pulled her into his arms, his mouth covering hers in a kiss of such desire that it nearly swept her mind clean of the wild story he'd just told her. And she surrendered to him, clung to him as his tongue explored her mouth and his hands slid down her body, his fingers sliding between her legs.

No, she had to get a hold of herself. To get a handle on what he was saying. *He thinks I am his lover reincarnated!*

But it was hard to think with his fingers teasing the outer lips of her cunt, sliding on the wetness he found there. He growled low in her ear.

"I need you now." His tongue traced the sensitive shell of her ear.

"Wait a minute!" Colleen wanted to ask more. But he was already moving them toward the bed. He swept her up in his arms and gently lowered her on the rumpled comforter before coming at her, eyes aglow. His cock jutted out proud and ready.

"But—"

Sean's kiss cut her off. He poured so much passion, so much fire into that kiss. More kisses for her shoulders, her breasts, as his hips and legs insinuated themselves between her thighs. Colleen was beyond speech and thought when she felt his cock slide past her outer lips, slide so easily into her waiting passage that was already a little sore from his loving.

Colleen wrapped herself around him, wanting his fierce possession and getting her fill as he teased and tormented her. His hand slid between their bodies to tease her swollen clit as his generous staff slid in and out of her at a determined pace. Colleen reveled in the way he filled her, stretched her. Her slick inner walls gripped his cock greedily with each thrust that sent waves of ecstasy coursing through her body.

Grasping her hips in his hands, he thrust every hard inch of his cock into her over and over. He brought her to orgasm several times, teasing her lips with his own, teasing her shoulder with his tongue which was something she'd always loved. His stamina was incredible and he kept at her until her thighs quivered around his, her body shaking from exhaustion.

And extreme satisfaction.

"Sean?" Colleen rested her head on his chest, draped her body over his. "You didn't finish the story. You didn't tell how you found out for sure that woman wasn't..."

Colleen stopped herself from saying *me.* She had little choice but to believe his story about being vampire. But she wasn't sure she was ready to believe that she was his reincarnated lover.

"I stalked her relentlessly, but she managed to evade me. She disappeared that night, left your father's farm to rot. What did she care? She'd gotten what she wanted. But she'd taken you away from me and I could never get past that."

"You're over two hundred years old then? Is that what you are saying?" Colleen finally made the connection as she pulled her head up to gaze into his eyes. "You said that you've followed this Sheehan person for decades. Did you—"

"Yes," Sean cut her off. "I sold myself to the darkness, found a vampire willing to take on a fledgling, just to destroy Regan Sheehan for taking from me the only thing I ever wanted. *You.*"

Colleen's heart squeezed at his words, at the endearments meant for the woman he believed her to be. The emotion in his eyes and his voice almost made her wish it *was* her that his words were meant for. To have a man love her so much...

"You *are* her," Sean replied to her thoughts. "And you came back to me. You don't remember now, but one day you will. I'm willing to wait. I have all the time in the world."

But Colleen didn't. She was just a human and humans didn't live forever.

"It is your choice," Sean deliberately answered her thoughts again. "I won't force you to join me in this life, but you can if you choose. And I can wish for that, try to convince you." His hand grabbed hers, pulled it down to the hard, hot column of his cock, ready, to her amazement, to go again. His smile was decidedly wicked. "I rather like the thought of convincing you of how good an eternity with me could be."

Me? A vampire? Colleen didn't even want to think about that now. She was so far beyond her experience tonight that she wouldn't even go there. But she couldn't stop herself from grinning. Okay, so she would have no trouble with the convincing part.

Colleen rose above him, straddling him, though where she got the strength after the night she'd had so far she couldn't say. Stroking his length in her hands, she watched his eyes flutter closed in pleasure at her touch. Colleen couldn't get enough of him, craved him between her legs. She impaled herself on him, filling herself with him and grinding her hips until the slow steady friction of their movements hit all the right spots within her.

Planting her hands on his chest, she moved on him at a pace all her own and he clutched her hips in his hands, urging her on. Sean was beautiful lying there beneath her, his cock buried inside her and she wanted to pleasure him, to ride him until he came hard.

But before she knew it, he'd taken control away from her, driving up into her center while her body milked him. Sean lifted his head to capture her nipples with his lips, the delicate teasing of his tongue driving her insane as he controlled the thrusting within her, pushing her to exquisite heights of ecstasy. Her hands were wild in his hair, on his back as he tormented her. Colleen held on as long as she could, he was *that* good, but finally her orgasm burst through her and he prolonged it with firm thrusts in just the right spot. Her pussy pulsed around him as she cried out his name over and over.

Sean rolled her onto her back, not done with her yet, continuing to drive into her like a vampire possessed. Colleen wouldn't have thought it possible to come again, but the friction of their bodies against her clit, the incredible feeling of being filled by him again and again proved quickly to be more than she could bear. When he climaxed, she went with him, hanging onto him as they rode out the storm of their passion.

CHAPTER 7

The phone ringing on the bedside table startled Colleen awake. She'd shot up in the bed and pressed the phone receiver to her ear before she ever realized it.

"Hello?" Colleen answered with her heart racing in her chest.

"Ms. O'Leary? This is the front desk. There is a Ms. Regina Starr here to see you," a cheerful voice announced.

Her new boss was there? *Well, hell!*

"Please tell her that I'll be down in just a few moments," Colleen replied.

The first rays of the sun filtered in through the windows, shafts of light falling across Sean's sleeping form next to her in the bed and she panicked. Couldn't the sunlight kill a vampire?

"Sean!" Colleen nudged him, hard. "Sean, wake up! It's morning! Sean, wake up, please!"

Blinking like a sleepy owl, he opened his eyes, smiled at her.

"Sean, the *sunlight*!" Colleen said meaningfully, jerking her thumb in the direction of the window.

Sean threw back his head and laughed. *Damn him!*

"You've seen too many movies, love." Sean leaned in to steal a kiss from her lips. "I struggled with the sunlight when I was reborn a vampire, but after so many years… I'm not as strong in the day, but I can get around just fine. I don't sleep in a coffin or anything."

Well, that would certainly help matters if she continued to see him. But there were so many other things to talk about, think about. How would anything work out between them? Would he want to make her a vampire? Would she have to become one herself to stay with him?

And she *did* want to see him again, she realized. She'd be crazy not to. A man who could love her as he did with that much stamina? Who *looked* like him?

Oh yeah.

Of course they'd have to talk about this idea of his that she was his reincarnated lover from two hundred years ago. How could she hope to compete with a woman long gone? She wanted him to see her for who she was, desire *her*.

Yes, she definitely wanted his desire.

But first things first. Her boss was waiting downstairs. Easing her sore body from the bed, Colleen headed for the shower. She could feel Sean's gaze on her as she walked away from the bed.

* * *

Sean had been strangely subdued when she'd gotten dressed and told him she was heading downstairs to finally meet her boss, but said nothing. Of course he'd kissed her senseless before she could make it out the door and as much as she would have liked to finish what he'd started in bed, she couldn't. But he'd let her go and hadn't asked or insisted to go with her. Perhaps not a bad thing considering the effect he had on her.

The lady at the front desk smiled at Colleen when she asked for Regina Starr and led her to a small meeting room. Colleen walked in and closed the door behind her. A woman sat alone in the room with her back to the door. But it was her long red, curly hair that had Colleen's heart hammering in her chest. A very familiar shade of red.

It was a dream. That's not a monster. That's just your new boss. Calm down!

But Colleen was shaking when the woman rose from her chair and turned to face her, a smile on her pretty face. The woman looked like she might be in her late thirties and she had bright blue eyes. But her smile didn't seem to reach her eyes. No, the woman's eyes rounded in surprise as they raked over Colleen from head to toe. Colleen knew in an instant the woman thought she recognized her just as Sean said he did.

Oh, shit.

"Ms. Starr?" Colleen tried to smile, play it off. Maybe it was just her imagination working overtime. "I'm Colleen O'Leary. Nice to meet you finally."

Regina Starr seemed to recovery quickly, held out a hand to Colleen. "Yes, I am glad to finally meet you, too."

Colleen was about to take the hand offered her when Sean's low, menacing voice stopped her. "Don't touch her."

Watching the woman's face, Colleen waited. Was this woman really her boss? Was Sean telling her the truth or was he completely insane? Either way she stood there, terrified. Either way she had reason to be afraid. At the very least of losing her job.

An annoyed smirk formed on Regina Starr's face. "This is getting old. Don't you have anything better to do?"

"Aside from killing you?" The controlled rage in Sean's voice forced a chill down Colleen's back. "No."

Regina's laughter was high and melodious. "You haven't managed to harm a hair on my head for over two hundred years. What makes you think you'll be able to do it now?"

"I beg to differ," Sean countered. "I was about to do quite a bit of harm to that stolen head the night before last at the gas station."

The gas station! Oh, my God! Colleen remembered now. She'd stopped at the gas station to get directions to the birthday party. A man had been choking a woman in the shadows next to the building. She could see Sean's face in her mind. *It had been him!* Colleen had not gotten a look at the woman, but she remembered her red hair trailing out behind her as she ran away.

"Perhaps." Regina's eyes turned to her, started to glow yellow. "I guess I should thank little Colleen for her help that night."

The de-icer. She'd sprayed Sean with it to free Regina. *Damn it!*

Her nightmare was realized as the woman's face shriveled and grayed until into a monstrous mask with enormous yellow fangs and black wizened skin. Colleen screamed and spun around to head for Sean. She'd made it two steps when she a long thick tentacle grabbed her, wrapped twice around her shaking form as it pulled her back towards Regina or whatever it was.

Sean's face was a study in rage as he stood watching them. "Let her go."

His voice was *too* calm and Colleen was terrified.

"She's mine," Regina hissed from behind her in voice that went from high and melodic to demonic possession. A long dark forked tongue shot out into Colleen's field of vision before licking the side of her face like a dog. "She's my bloodline."

"You're wrong," Sean's voice was barely above a whisper.

His gray eyes met Colleen's and her heart thundered in her chest at the determination in them. He was getting ready to *do* something. *Oh, shit!*

"She's *mine!*" Sean's voice thundered through the room and in a flash he shot through the air in the direction of Regina.

Colleen was hurled through the air like a rag doll and struck the wall with a force that jarred her bones. All hell broke loose around her, the sound like a dump truck crashing through the room, and she pulled herself up from the floor, bruised and hurting, to see them battling on the ceiling.

On the ceiling! Sean fought a creature that looked like an ancient dragon with tentacles, both of them defying gravity as they battled to the death. The creature lashed her tentacles out at Sean, their sound like the cracking of whips. One lash split the denim of his jeans at his thigh, striping his flesh. But the long line of blood disappeared in an instant, the wound completely healed.

The lady from the front desk of the hotel rushed in with wide eyes and quickly rushed back out as Sean grabbed the creature by one of its wings and slung it against the wall opposite of Colleen. Its body collapsed like a bat's, but in an instant it was on its feet and heading straight for her, snarling and hissing.

Sean fell to the floor, landing perfectly on his feet in front of Colleen on the table at the center of the room. She could feel the power, the rage emanating from his body as she backed against the wall.

"Now, Regan, you die."

Sean flew at the creature, his motion so quick Colleen hardly knew what had happened until she saw him beating the monster with powerful blows into the floor. Another tentacle whipped across his chest, slicing his shirt and skin open, but he seemed not to notice as he repeatedly drove his fists into the creature like a man possessed. When the monster started screaming, Colleen covered her ears, unable to bear the sound. Those cries became more frantic, more shrill as Sean locked his powerful arms around the creature's head and with furious strength ripped it from the creature's body.

Sean's head shot up at the sound of the police sirens outside. "Colleen! Are you all right?"

Colleen nodded, still trying to catch her breath from what she'd seen. She didn't immediately notice that Sean had appeared beside her, pulling her into the safety of his arms. No, she was too busy watching the body of the creature bubble and melt, sliding down the wall like black oil.

"You're sure you're all right?" Sean cupped her face and forced her to look at him.

"Yes," Colleen swallowed hard, her eyes gazing up into his.

"I have to leave now," he explained gently. "This room will be crawling with police officers in just a couple of minutes. Can you imagine the field day the forensic scientists will have with that? Or would have with *me* for that matter?"

Colleen's gaze darted to the messy remains of the creature back to him.

"I want you to be with me, Colleen." Sean's lips brushed hers in a kiss of infinite tenderness. "I don't care if you never remember the other life we shared. I just want to share *this* life with you. If you'll have me. I'll always keep you safe. I'll satisfy every need and desire you'll ever have, you know I can."

His strong hand, stained with the creature's blood, lifted to her cheek. His eyes were dark with desire as they searched hers.

"I don't ever want to live without you again," Sean whispered. "Will you have me?"

Colleen's heart squeezed in her chest at the raw emotion in his eyes.

Sean had told her he was a vampire and he was. He'd told her he would keep her safe and he had, saving her from the creature who'd stalked her, that he claimed had killed her in another life. Could it have been true? Hadn't Regina Starr looked at her as if she knew her before she'd turned monstrous? Hadn't she made reference to the fact that Sean had been following her for two hundred years, bent on destroying her?

And if all that were true, could she *really* be his love born again?

The sound of footsteps racing up the hall drew their attention to the closed door.

It's now or never. Make the call.

"Yes," Colleen whispered. "I want to be with you."

EPILOGUE

Dublin was alive with sounds and people and Sean smiled as Colleen pulled him into a pub called The Vaults. It was like stepping back in time for him with its charming brick archways and shining wooden floors. She made her way through the throng of people around the bar to another room, following the sound of a lovely ballad and he followed her. When they reached the room where people crowded around the Irish folk band performing there, Colleen smiled brightly.

And Sean turned hard as a stone. Her smile always did that to him.

It'd been months since their first night together and that terrible morning with Regan Sheehan, but his Colleen had proven to be remarkably resilient and open-minded. They'd managed to avoid police questioning about the incident long enough to collect her belongings and get out of town. They'd rented a house in the states for a while, but Ireland called to him, so they'd moved there in the last month.

It was his home. *Their* home.

He knew Colleen doubted his story that they'd loved each other before, claimed she had no memories of it. From what he could tell from the flashes he read in her mind what she said was true. But he wouldn't give up hope that one day she'd remember.

She was with him *now*, wasn't she? Sean kept her in his bed as much as possible and when they weren't there, she was content to travel Ireland with him, to listen to his stories and explanations of his world, the vampires. What he knew of it anyway.

Colleen still worked at her computer now and again, but to Sean's amusement, her time at the damnable contraption grew shorter and shorter. He wanted her busy mind on him, her hands on him.

He turned harder. It was time to go.

Sean wrapped an arm about her waist and whispered in her ear. "I want to be inside you now."

Colleen grinned at him impishly and shook her head as the band began another ballad.

"Not until I hear this song. It's my favorite," she explained.

So it was. Sean stared at her in amazement. It had been *Eileen's* favorite song.

Colleen began to sing along with the band, the ballad of a simple girl and the boy who loved her. She knew all the words, her singing voice high and beautiful. Sean remembered her singing on her father's farm just that way so many years ago.

"When did you learn to speak in Gaelic?" Sean asked her meaningfully.

She froze where she stood, her lovely face paling and her eyes rounding in surprise.

"I don't know," she whispered.

Sean pulled her into her arms in the middle of the crowded room and took her mouth in a passionate kiss. Overjoyed at that promising glimmer of hope, he led her from the room. The night was just beginning and he wanted to be inside of her.

His love...

ELEGANT

CHAPTER 1

Ella Kent shoved aside the empty platter and made a grab for the double banana split her friend had ordered for her birthday. Richard Shelton, her best friend since high school, gave her that little smirk that let her know there'd be a discussion before he handed over the dessert. He pulled it back across the wooden tabletop until it was out of her reach. Something he might not have managed so easily if her arms were a little longer or the table was a little narrower.

Ah, who was she kidding? She was fat. The spare tire around her waist was the biggest reason she couldn't reach that scrumptious bit of chocolate-topped heaven, and she knew it.

"Oh, no you don't." Richard pulled the dessert further out of reach when she tried again. "Not until you tell me what happened earlier."

"Nothing happened earlier." Ella tried to deny it.

But her friend had always been able to read her far too easily. Richard shook his head, his sharp eyes pinning her in the chair.

"If nothing happened," he said, "why did you stop at Godiva's after work?"

Ella cringed. She'd seen him playing the violin in the window of his apartment when she came home, but didn't think he had seen her. And she'd given herself kudos for smuggling the enormous bag of chocolate candy into her apartment without him seeing her. *Damn him!*

"It's my birthday," she pointed out, knowing she wouldn't get anywhere. "Can't I treat myself for my birthday?"

"For one birthday? Or ten?"

Frowning at him, she slumped back into her chair.

"All right." Ella blew out a frustrated sigh. He was right. She was celebrating her birthday; she was compensating. She'd had a bad day. And he wouldn't give up until she admitted he was right. "It was a hectic afternoon, that's all."

"Hectic," Richard repeated.

"Well, yeah," she began. "Lunch was busy and it never really slowed down after that. Plus Rudy fired the new part-time cook."

Richard's dark brows knitted. "Which one was he?"

"The one who called me Ella Kent the Elephant," Ella replied flatly.

He nodded, but didn't say anything.

Watching Richard nonchalantly sipping wine, she realized how lucky she was to have him as a friend. He accepted her, just the way she was, which was something the rest of the world struggled with. He never looked at her with pity or revulsion or any of the equally annoying emotions in between that she was so accustomed to from everyone else.

Sure, he drove her crazy sometimes harping at her about diets and exercise. But all his advice and nagging came from a place where he wanted to help her.

"Why did he get fired?" Richard asked.

"Mostly for swiping tips," Ella offered.

"Mostly. But what he actually got fired for was…" He held out his hand, palm up, to prompt her for the answer.

"Well, it was stupid really." She felt uncomfortable now. And she shouldn't. She had no secrets from Richard. But the incident earlier in the café where she worked bothered her, and that was something considering the tough hide she'd developed from years of fat jokes. "He took my uniform out of my locker and drew on it."

Richard's brows lifted. He patiently waited for her to continue.

"He drew on the back of my uniform. It was supposed to look like a brand on my butt. Like I was a steer or something. I didn't know it was there when I started my shift. Really funny, huh?"

The concern she read in her friend's eyes nearly had her in tears again, but she fought it. She really should be immune to such childishness by now. But it had been hard today. She'd been laughed at for two hours before one of her regulars pointed out the cruel joke that had been played on her.

She'd held onto her composure and had even tried to laugh with them. But Rudy, the owner, found it a convenient excuse to fire the cook who'd been nothing but trouble since they'd hired him. And that had only made matters worse for Ella. Half the restaurant staff thought she'd whined to Rudy about the joke, causing him to get fired, while the other half felt sorry for her. And she hated pity more than anything.

Ella somehow made it through the day and headed straight for Godiva's the moment she left work, as she always did when she was feeling low. She'd be the first one to admit she had a psychological dependence on chocolate, sugar, cake frosting. And the lower she felt, the more she ate.

"It's okay," she told him. "He's gone now, right?"

"That's right."

Tears gathered in her eyes anyway.

"You okay?" Richard reached across the table for her hand.

She nodded. "It's just not how I envisioned spending my thirtieth birthday. I guess I always thought I'd be spending it with the man of my dreams, maybe a couple of kids, in a nice, big house in the country. But here I am—still in Chicago, big as a house, celebrating my birthday with my gay best friend."

"Dashing, gay best friend," he corrected with a wink, making her chuckle despite the sad realization.

And then she remembered the other item she'd picked up on her way home. A novelty item she'd bought from a street vendor at the small carnival she'd run across at Navy Pier.

"I bought something else," she threw out to change the subject. "There was a small carnival at the pier."

"I hadn't noticed." Richard slid the banana split across the table to her. "What did you buy?"

"A magic potion." Ella winked at him as she snatched up her spoon and dug into the chocolate and nut-covered treat with delight. "This is wonderful. Thank you!"

Richard waved away the thank you.

"A magic potion, huh?" After draining his wine glass, he eyed her curiously as she ate. "What is it supposed to do?"

"Make me beautiful." *If only,* she thought. "Well, for only thirty days and only if I say the little verse on the jar nine times and make a wish."

"And if there's a harvest moon, a one-legged nun walking a goat by the Sears Tower, and—"

"I know." Ella laughed. "But this Gypsy lady had such a good spiel, Richard. She told me the potion only truly worked for special people and she could see I was one of those—the whole nine yards."

Richard shook his head. "There's a good reason to buy things. I'm glad you're not car shopping."

"Oh, stop," Ella managed between bites. "It was fun."

"They didn't have a potion that would conjure a gorgeous hunk, did they?" Her friend's eyes sparkled in mischief. "Now, if she was pitching that…"

"I'd have beaten you to it," she assured him.

After a laugh, he said, "Ah, well, at least it'll make an interesting addition to your knick-knack shelf."

She finished her banana split and considered that suggestion. It probably *would* be quite a conversation piece for when she had company over. But she was lucky to have company outside of Richard, and her family who only made it in once a year.

Well, I could always try the potion, she thought. *Yeah, right.* It would be her luck to end up in the hospital. The fat chick getting her stomach pumped. She could just hear the jokes on that one. "This will take a while," they'd say.

"I'm going to the restroom before we go," Ella told him as she clumsily slid out of the booth.

Concern still clouded her friend's gaze as he looked up at her.

"Did you rent anything for tonight?" she asked hopefully.

His face split into a wide grin. "Of course. A romantic comedy with sex and good-lookin' boys."

"Wowsa!" Ella laughed. "My kind of movie! I'll hurry."

Ella turned and bustled toward the ladies room. But before she could turn the corner to reach the door, she collided with a large, solid form. The impact knocked her off balance and she landed squarely on her generous butt, hard. Sharp pain raced through her back and legs as she sat on the floor stunned.

"I'm sorry," a deep voice pierced her disorientation. "Are you all right?"

She gazed up into the bluest eyes she'd ever seen. The man was tall with black hair that framed his face in long layers and his shoulders looked as wide as church doors. Everything about him, from the hard planes of his handsome face to the black leather jacket he wore with faded jeans, told her that he was a man used to the world and well-used by it.

Ella nodded, pulled her gaze away. "I think so."

"Let me help you up."

Shaking her head, she said, "No, I can—"

"I insist."

She hated this part. Wasn't it bad enough she was already a spectacle in the crowded restaurant? Fat girl down. But now he'd try to haul her up from the floor, he wouldn't be able to, and she wouldn't be able to return to her favorite restaurant for months.

But he managed the task easily. Kneeling by her side, he wrapped a strong, muscular arm around her back and cupped her elbow with his other hand. She was back on her feet in an instant, mesmerized by the gorgeous stranger standing so close to her. He smelled wonderful, earthy and warm, and his hard body pressing against hers was a new and unfamiliar experience. It messed with her insides.

"Th-thank you," she managed, gazing up at him shyly.

"You're sure you're okay?"

He had an accent. *Irish,* she thought. And his eyes were warm and friendly. Not a trace of mockery or pity to be found. Her heart melted. What would she give to have a man like that in her life? Someone gorgeous, kind, and nonjudgmental…

"I'm fine," she muttered.

"El? Are you okay?" Richard's tone was one of worry until he spotted her rescuer. Then he smiled brightly. "Oh, hello."

The good-looking man nodded briefly at her friend's enthusiastic greeting but nothing more and she knew a moment's relief. *Well, at least he isn't gay.* She could fantasize about him.

"Your meals are on the house tonight," he said as he stepped back from Ella. "Who's your waitress tonight?"

"Tall and skinny," Richard described. "Dark hair, crossed eyes."

The man nodded knowingly. "Crystal. I'll let her know."

"It's her birthday, too," Richard tipped his head toward Ella.

Not knowing what he hoped to accomplish with that, she shot her friend the dirtiest look she could manage.

But the handsome man stepped into her line of vision as he headed out, and stopped before her with a lazy half-smile on his handsome face.

"Happy birthday," he bade her softly.

And then he was gone. But Ella could still feel his hard body pressed to hers, could still smell him. And the sound of his deep voice, well, that would be running through her head deep into the night.

"He is fine." Richard watched him walk away, too.

"He truly is," Ella said longingly.

They both watched until he'd disappeared from sight. Then Richard said, "Let's go."

*   *   *

Ella stared out of her apartment window with the scene in the restaurant playing over and over in her mind like a favorite movie. She didn't even mind the part where she fell; she'd abandoned pride long ago. All she could remember was the man who'd come to her rescue, and the beauty of his face, his voice.

And his kindness. It was almost as if he hadn't seen her as an enormous woman he'd knocked off her feet. It had been a heart-stopping moment. She couldn't imagine what it would be like to have him look at her with love in his deep blue eyes, with admiration.

To have him look at her like she was beautiful.

In an instant, she snatched her purse from the sofa where she'd dumped it when she and Richard returned from the restaurant. She pulled out empty candy wrappers, food coupons, lipsticks, keys. Ella began to panic until she spotted the object of her search nestled in the worn lining at the bottom of her purse.

The small jar she'd purchased from the Gypsy woman was glass with a cork top. The word "beauty" had been hand-written on a paper label on the jar that contained a dark green substance. It sure didn't look very appetizing.

Turning the jar in her hands, she began to read the tiny writing on the back of the label:

Drink all of this elixir at once by the light of the moon and, until the same moon returns, you will be changed. Make your heart's wish and say nine times, May my beauty inside be my beauty outside.

She knew it was crazy to even consider it. Of course the old Gypsy woman had been convincing and mysterious. Like Richard said, the woman had only wanted to sell her something.

And yet... Well, it was fun to dream. If she drank it, what was the worst thing that could happen? Well, if it were poison, she could die, she supposed. But likely, if she drank it, nothing would change; nothing would happen at all.

Like an excited child, she made her way to the kitchen for a corkscrew. She'd never been handy with little tools, but sheer determination got the cork out of that jar. The pleasant scent of flowers and spring rain floated up from the jar.

With a delighted laugh, she lifted the jar, tipping it to and fro to see that the contents were fluid and didn't appear too thick. And she had to drink it by the light of the moon, so she carried it back to her living room, pulled opened the curtains wide to reveal a full moon glowing in the sky overhead.

Well, here goes...

And, with a prayer that she wouldn't die of stupidity, she put the jar to her lips and downed the potion in a few great gulps. The taste was not unpleasant—minty and almost medicinal.

Now for a wish.

Instantly, an image of the handsome stranger from the restaurant filled her mind and her wish was made. Just once she'd like to know what it felt like to have someone like him to look at her as if she were someone special.

To finish the instructions, she repeated the verse from the label nine times, slowing down on the last repetition. In the silence of her apartment, she waited as she uttered the last word.

She didn't know what she expected to happen. Lightning bolts from the sky? A magical transformation with colorful smoke rising from the floor?

Nothing happened, and she felt no different.

Then she laughed. It had been fun. For the ten minutes or so she was opening the jar and completing the spell, she'd believed in magic.

It had felt good to do something different tonight because, usually, nothing ever changed for Ella. Every day she woke up alone and took the bus to her job at the café. All day she served the same meals to the same customers, smiling at the stories they'd already told. There were the jokes and slurs about her appearance, and she let those go by. Much worse was the journey back home to an empty apartment with only her television and food to keep her company.

But there's Richard, she thought fondly. What would she ever do without him?

Ella put the empty jar on the coffee table next to half-empty bowl of popcorn she'd shared with Richard earlier and sighed.

My thirtieth birthday. Well, it had been more than just another day, hadn't it? Her friend took her out for a nice dinner, she was knocked over by the most handsome man she'd ever laid eyes on, and she'd drank a magic potion she'd bought from a Gypsy that was supposed to make her beautiful.

Well, it would take more than a Gypsy's potion to make Ella Kent the Elephant beautiful, she thought as she snagged up the bag of chocolate candies she bought earlier and headed for bed.

It would take a miracle.

CHAPTER 2

Ella stretched as she slowly began to awaken. The sun shone brightly through the filmy curtains of her bedroom window and she fairly leapt from the bed in panic. The clock on the nightstand by her bed said it was half past eight! She should have been up two hours ago. *Rudy will be pissed!*

But the whirlwind of thoughts about being an hour late for work halted all at once as she glanced down.

Oh, my God, Ella thought as she reeled in shock. *What the hell happened?* Her body was... Well, it was...gone! Not literally of course, but it was certainly not the healthy two hundred and seventy five pounds of Ella that she'd always known and loved.

She ran to the bathroom and was frozen by the sight that greeted her in the mirror over the sink. Another woman's face stared back at her with her perfect mouth gaped open and her blue eyes wide in amazement.

Her hands flew to her face, verifying what the mirror told her. Her fingers traced the smooth contours of her face. The supple skin fit snugly against her cheekbones and jaw. Gone were the pockets of flesh she was accustomed to on both sides of her face and under her chin. Her hands glided down the smooth line of her neck, not finding the pad of flesh that usually hung there, but a smooth, slim column.

Leaning closer to the mirror, she stared at her altered reflection. Her eyes were the same at least—blue, but nothing extraordinary. But the rest of her face... *Dear Lord!* Was that how she looked as a thin woman?

She looked like the women in the fashion magazines who she'd always envied. Her face was pretty, all delicate, perfect angles and smooth, white skin. Her nose was slim and perfectly straight; her chin softly rounded. Her lips were full with that bee-stung look that had been all the rage for ages now, and that was something because her lips had been the thinnest thing about her since childhood.

Then she noticed her hair. Ella's hair had been her one good feature, naturally blonde and heavy. But even it was different; longer than it had been last night when she went to bed. Instead of the shoulder-length bob she normally wore, her hair hung in silky waves that fell past her shoulders to midway down her back.

My back! How long had it been since she'd been able to see her shoulder blades, her waist? Shutting the bathroom door with an anxious slam, she gazed at herself in the door's full-length mirror she seldom used.

Ella's mouth fell open again. The body she saw in the mirror was definitely not hers. She had ankles! And they were attached to long, slender legs that were smooth and toned. Turning to look over her shoulder she saw the back of herself in the mirror, and saw that those legs ended in a firm, well-rounded backside. *Hell, it looks as good as J. Lo's!*

Facing forward again, she hauled up the enormous nightshirt that was her favorite, pulling it over her head to reveal a truly glorious body. Her panties were missing—had probably fallen off—so she saw everything—the flat abdomen, the faint lines of her ribs, the full, shapely breasts that were just perfect for this body, but that would never fit into her double D bra.

Holding her arms out to her sides, she admired their long, slim lines. Even her fingers were slender, her nails clear and shiny.

What the hell had happened?

The potion!

Still naked, she ran into her living room to find the empty jar she'd bought from the lady at the carnival right where she'd left it. She read and reread the writing on the label. Yes, the woman had told her it was a magic potion and to follow the instructions.

It was supposed to be a novelty. It wasn't supposed to actually work!

Her mind spun. *Is this real? Or is it a dream?*

That's it, she thought, and she grasped a bit of skin on one of her new arms and pinched hard. She winced at the pain, but nothing changed. She didn't wake up again in her bed. She was still naked in someone else's body in the middle of her living room. *Oh, dear God!*

She hurried into her bedroom, snatched her blue robe from the foot of her bed and wrapped it about herself tightly as she headed out of her apartment. In seconds, she stood before Richard's apartment door down the hall, banging on it for all she was worth.

"Richard!"

He wouldn't be awake yet. And she could tell from the grumpy look on his face when he opened the door that he'd just crawled out of bed to answer the door.

"Yes?" His voice was tight and low. But if he saw anything amiss he took great pains not to show it.

"Well?" she asked waiting for the shock to register on his face.

But it didn't. His eyes, barely open from sleep, raked her from head to toe. He shook his head.

"You've got the wrong apartment," he mumbled and slammed the door in her face.

"Richard!" she cried in frustration. "It's me! Ella!"

After a couple of seconds, the door was yanked open and she was treated to one of his rare glares before he looked behind her, up and down the hallway. With an angry shake of his head, he slammed the door again.

"Richard! Open the door!" she demanded.

"Look—" His tone turned nasty as he pulled the door open again. "—I don't know what you're up to but you'd better leave or I—"

"Richard," she cut him off, pressing a hand to her chest. "It's me. Ella."

Obviously losing patience, he folded his arms across his chest.

"I hear Ella, but I don't see Ella," he said flatly.

"I know," she tried to explain. "You've got to—"

"Ella would already be at work by now," he pointed out.

"Richard, I overslept," she explained hurriedly. "You've got to help me. I drank that potion last night and—"

"Whoa!" Richard held up a hand to stop her. "Potion?"

"You remember? I told you about it last night at O'Malley's. I bought it at the carnival at Navy Pier."

His dark brows knitted as he processed her words. The confusion on his face was easy to read.

"I remember Ella telling me about a potion she'd bought—"

"I'm Ella!" she insisted.

Her friend's eyes locked with hers for a long moment before they moved over her face. "If you *are* Ella, tell me something only Ella would know."

She knew a moment's panic, but it didn't take long for her scrambling mind to come up with the hard evidence to convince her friend.

"You went to our senior prom with a *girl.*" She deliberately emphasized the word "girl." "Her name was Mary Madison Mathers. And she—"

Before she could finish, Richard grabbed her by the front of her loose robe and pulled her into the privacy of his apartment. Her startled friend stared at Ella as if she had two heads with six eyes between them as he closed his door.

"Ella?"

"It's me, Richard." She willed him to believe her. "I'm just as shocked—"

"Wait." He frowned. "If this is some kind of joke…"

"Who would help me with any kind of joke?" she wanted to know. "You're my only friend."

Shoving his hands into the pockets of his own robe, he nodded. "True."

"Richard, you have to help me!" she begged him as she began to pace. "What am I going to do? If you didn't recognize me, you know they won't at work!"

He shrugged. "Call in sick."

That stopped her. "For thirty days? I'm going to lose my job," she moaned. "My clothes won't fit! How am I going to buy something to wear with no job?"

"My God," Her friend's stare told her that the enormity of her situation had finally begun to sink into his recently awakened mind. His eyes were dark and serious as they fastened on her. "The first thing we have to do is find that Gypsy woman."

Okay, that makes sense, she decided, thinking it was the first thing since she'd awakened that had.

"I'll go find something of mine for you to wear." Richard sprung into action.

Ella smiled. She knew Richard would think of something.

"Richard, thank you." She followed him to his bedroom in her nervousness. "If she can change me back—"

"Change you back?" Richard slung open the door of his large closet. "Hell! I want some of that stuff!"

* * *

It was the day after Ella's thirtieth birthday and her life had been turned upside down. She sat in the same booth at O'Malley's she and Richard had occupied the night before, eating an enormous plate of spaghetti. The comfort she normally felt from her favorite restaurant didn't come.

The carnival had disappeared from Navy Pier without a trace and the Gypsy woman with it. Richard had been crestfallen about not having the opportunity to try the potion. She didn't tell him as much, but she'd been relieved that he'd missed his chance. What good was it to be beautiful for thirty days when, during that time, life as you knew it fell apart?

After they'd grown tired of asking people if they knew anything about the carnival that had been in town, they went to the café where Ella worked. Against Richard's advice, she tried to explain to Rudy what had happened. The man she'd worked for for some eleven years not only laughed and told her to get out, but he'd tried to grab her ass as well! And he'd told her to tell Ella when she saw her that she was fired.

She would've lost her job anyway. Unless she was in the hospital with tubes up her nose, Rudy would never buy she was too sick to work for an entire month.

Finally, Richard had to leave her to go get ready for symphony practice. She'd waved him on. At least he still had a job to go to.

What a damned mess!

"Now what's such a sad look doing on such a beautiful face?"

Ella's heart began to pound in her chest at the sound of that familiar voice. She figured the whole restaurant could likely hear the loud thumping as she gazed up at him, the man who had felled her last night and haunted her dreams. There he stood in all his beauty, his black hair smoothed back from his handsome face by a recent shower and his appreciative male eyes moving over her face and body.

She stared at him with her mouth hanging open. It was all she could do.

His deep blue eyes locked with hers.

"Do I know you?" he asked quietly, studying her.

Ella swallowed hard. Did he recognize her?

"I've seen *you* here before," was all Ella was going to say.

And it worked. Any recognition in his amazing blue eyes melted away as he slid into the booth across from her.

"I'll have my eyes checked." He melted her heart with a devilish flash of white teeth and his subtle Irish accent. "I'm sure I'd remember you if I'd seen you here before."

Her face went up in flames under his intent stare. It wasn't that she was unaccustomed to being stared at. She most definitely was. But she was used to being stared at with pity or amazement...or worse, mockery.

Men had been eying her all morning in unmasked appreciation. And when she'd finally noticed, it had been quite startling. But the way this man's eyes caressed her with deliberate intimacy was terrifying. It made her want to run, from him—from the electricity coursing through her that tightened her nipples into hard twin points and created a delicate ache between her thighs. It was so easy to imagine the feeling of his strong fingers stoking that fire down below, gliding on her wetness to tantalize her clit...

"I've embarrassed you." He laughed softly, the low rumble twisting her insides even more. "But you haven't yet answered my first question."

"Why I look down? You wouldn't believe me if I told you."

"Give it a try," he prompted as he sat back in the seat, his smile never wavering.

It was clear he wasn't giving up. What was she supposed to tell him? *It all started when I bought a magic potion from a Gypsy at Navy Pier. I drank the potion and made a wish—which involved you by the way—and—*

Her wish! The realization that he was here, with her, as she had wished hit her like a blast of hot wind. *Of course!* If the potion had made her beautiful as it had promised, why wouldn't she get her wish, too? Wasn't the man she'd dreamt of all night here gazing at her as if she were the most desirable woman he'd ever seen? Wasn't that what she'd wished for? To know what that was like?

Ella smiled, fighting the urge to laugh out loud in delight. *This man, this beautiful, sexy man is all mine for thirty days.* This was her wish come true. *Oh, the possibilities!*

"Now that's much better," he broke in on her thoughts. "That's a smile to make a man lightheaded."

"I can't help it," she admitted while excitement coursed through her body. "I'm so glad you're here."

His eyes darkened like a night sky as he leaned forward. "Are you now?"

"I am. You're just what I wished for."

"Am I?" His expression had taken on a predatory quality.

The awkwardness Ella felt only lasted a moment. Wasn't she a grown woman with desires and needs? She wasn't a virgin, thank goodness for that, but she couldn't boast much more experience than one. Two uninspiring attempts at sex were all she could claim and both had been early in her twenties. One had been a skinny boy she'd met at the café who'd had no idea of what foreplay meant. The other had been an older man, who'd conveniently forgotten to tell her he was married. The foreplay with him had been good—he had done incredible things with his tongue—but when it came to doing the deed, he'd blown his wad after only half a dozen strokes.

But she had fantasies. Oh, did she have fantasies! Deep in the night she had dreamt of lovers touching her, fondling her breasts, teasing her clitoris, and the pleasure of joining her body with theirs. And her dreams of *this* man last night, his hands on her body, his *mouth* on her body. Ella had imagined wrapping herself around him, going down on him…

But as she returned the intense gaze of the man who far surpassed any dream lover she could conjure, it wasn't lost on her that she could make some of those fantasies happen. Why shouldn't she? She only had thirty days. At the end of that month, the memories would be all that Ella Kent the Elephant would have.

Her mind was made up.

"You are. Otherwise, you wouldn't have anything to do with me."

If that had caught him off guard, he did an amazing job of concealing it. Or maybe it was the spell controlling him.

"You're wrong about that." His voice was low and calm.

"Do you always pay such attention to people in this restaurant?" Ella teased.

"It's my restaurant. I'm one of its owners, and I want my customers to be satisfied."

"And you give all of your patrons such personal attention?"

"Just the ones I want."

Ella's thighs squeezed together against the wave of lust—no other word for it—that his words brought on. Moisture flooded the pants she wore. His invitation was clear.

What? You're going to just leave with him? Have sex with him? You don't even know his name! A voice a lot like her mother's droned on and on in her head. *Well, that isn't anything new,* she mused. The only difference was that nagging voice usually addressed her eating habits. *Do you really need that donut? Isn't that your third piece of pie?*

Her mother would condemn her for a slut if she knew what she was about to do. Ella squirmed in her seat under her gorgeous stranger's gaze, her body quickly winning the passion battle. *What did it matter what anyone thought?* Who would recognize her? And once she went back to normal, who the hell would believe her?

"You want me?" She pitched her voice low, enjoying her newly discovered confidence.

"You require proof?"

"I'd like proof." She met his gaze squarely.

In an instant, he'd captured her hand in his own, his eyes ocean deep as he slid to the edge of his seat.

His erection strained the front of his jeans and had Ella shivering in delicious anticipation.

"Let's go."

Ella didn't know if she'd leapt to her feet or he dragged her out of the booth, and she didn't care. Before she knew it, they were out the door, his grip tight on her hand. She had a difficult time matching the pace of his long legs as they ate up the sidewalk, but somehow she managed. She was breathless by the time they reached his sleek, black Jaguar.

Holding the door open, he motioned her inside.

She stopped. There was one thing she really should know.

"What's your name?"

His tight chuckle told her he might have laughed in earnest if he hadn't been in sorry shape. "Ian Clayton."

CHAPTER 3

Ian Clayton lived in Manhattan and had what appeared to be a beautiful apartment. Ella only caught as glimpse of it as he slammed the door behind her and backed her up against it, standing so close, yet not touching her. His breath was ragged, and warm as it caressed her face. The intensity of his gaze captured hers and her heart thundered in her chest.

Each breath she took had her hard, sensitive nipples chafing against the sweater she wore. She wanted to be free of the borrowed sweater and the slacks clinging damply to the vee between her legs. Ella wanted nothing more than to wrap herself around him and burrow into the heat of his hard, ready body.

No turning back now, she thought.

"You're the most beautiful thing I've ever seen," he whispered, catching a lock of her gleaming hair in his rough fingers. "Who are you?"

She could barely find the voice to speak. Spell or no spell, it was the most magical moment of her entire life.

"Ella Kent," she managed.

Strong fingers tipped her chin back up, forcing her to meet his eyes again. "What?"

"Ella Kent," she said slowly.

Some emotion crossed his handsome features, but he said nothing. She'd have been uncomfortable with the silence if she hadn't already wanted to jump out of her skin from the nearness of him. The smell of warm skin and man, and the heat from his body had her tingling with an unfamiliar awareness.

"You know…rhymes with elephant," she tried with a half-hearted attempted to laugh.

His smile had her heart leaping, the fire down low burning hotter.

"I thought you said 'elegant.'"

Ian lowered his head and took her mouth with a gentleness she hadn't expected. His firm, sensuous lips caressed hers slowly, savoring her, as his hands sank into her hair, holding her in place for his skillful exploration. Ella drowned in that kiss, clutching his leather jacket for support because she didn't know how much longer her shaking knees would hold her up.

He deepened the kiss at her willing response.

Her hands sought the flat planes of his rock solid chest as his tongue seductively glided in and around her mouth, matching the rhythm of the hard thigh he'd wedged between her legs. The incredible heat of him pressed against her belly, nudging gently in a deliberate rhythm had her senses spiraling out of control. She clung to him as the craving built, pushing against his erection, trying to capture his taunting thigh between her own.

His lips burned a trail from her mouth to the column of her throat and she gasped as his tongue teased the sensitive flesh below her left ear. He captured her ear lobe, suckling it gently before his tongue began to trace the delicate shell of her inner ear. One of his hands slid beneath her sweater in the same instant, finding her bare breast. His fingers gently played at her tight nipple, making her want to scream for relief from the storm of sensations.

"I want you now, Elegant," his voice was a course whisper in her ear.

Elegant. She liked that.

Ella cried out when his hand left her breast and he pulled his leg free from hers, but she didn't have long to ponder it as he swept her off her feet. Even in the heat of the moment, it wasn't lost on Ella that it was probably the first time since early childhood that someone had been able to carry her anywhere.

He headed through the spacious apartment and into a large, masculine bedroom in shades of tan and black. Gorgeous mahogany furniture was strategically placed around the enormous four-poster bed at its center. The leafy pattern of the tan-and-black comforter raced up at her as he nearly flung her onto the center of his bed.

Ian climbed onto the bed, stalking her. His blue eyes pinned her in place as he stripped away the leather jacket to reveal an impressive display of muscled arms, straining the black T-shirt he wore beneath. She wanted him to strip away the shirt, but he came straight toward her. The hunger in his eyes wiped her mind clean of anything else.

Richard's black-and-silver sweater was pulled over her head in an instant and then Ian's mouth reclaimed hers. Ella was treated to another slow, tantalizing kiss as his body lowered deliciously onto hers. He nudged her thighs apart with his own and began to press himself against her in a relentless rhythm. His kiss had her squirming in desire beneath him, straining to get closer. Her hands were wild on him as he took his time, torturing her.

The thick locks of his hair were cool and sleek between her fingers. Her hands skimmed beneath his shirt to slide on the sweat-dampened skin of his torso, reveling in the sheer power of the muscular body all around her.

With a low growl, he captured her wrists and pinned them to the bed on either side of her head. "You won't hurry me, you little devil." There was a hint of laughter in his voice. "No, you won't hurry me at all."

And he meant what he said. No matter how she twisted her slim wrists in his grip, he wouldn't let go. He took his time, tasting her lips, trailing kisses across her cheek until his hot breath was back in her ear. And all the while, he nudged at the damp vee between her thighs with his heat and hardness.

"You want me so badly, don't you, Elegant?" His voice and his tongue played in her ear. "You're on fire. I can't wait to be inside you. I'm going to fuck you for hours."

Moaning, she pressed her body up against his as close as she could. It was all she could do.

Ella did cry out when his lips closed around her nipple. His tongue swirled casual circles around the taut tip as the motion of his hips stopped. He seemed not to notice when she began bucking against him, trying to get him to continue the delicate grinding. He grinned at her impishly before his mouth began to work on her other breast, letting her know he'd deliberately stopped.

When finally he lifted his head and released her wrists, she pulled his mouth to hers ferociously, kissing him for all she was worth. Ella caught his full lower lip between her own and nipped playfully at it. She drew a moan from him when she coaxed his mouth open and slid her tongue inside to taste him. Her hands tore at his shirt before they drifted down the muscular abdomen to the huge bulge in his jeans. Her fingers had barely begun to explore the thick length of him beneath the coarse denim when he grabbed her wrists again and dragged her to the top of the bed.

"I won't be lasting long with you doing that," he said matter-of-factly. He pulled off his shirt in a single fluid motion, dazzling Ella with the hairless planes of his upper body. She was so caught up in admiring him that she didn't immediately realize he was binding her wrists to the bedpost with the shirt.

"Wait, I—"

Ian silenced her with a gentle kiss.

"Trust me," he whispered, his tongue sliding back into her mouth. "Trust me."

Ella was breathless when his hands began to work the fastenings of Richard's black trousers. If Ian noticed that she wore men's clothing, he said nothing as he pulled her legs free and grinned in appreciation at the fact she wore no panties.

God, what must he think?

Unceremoniously, he pulled her thighs apart and settled himself between them, sitting on the bed. Now her nervousness blended with her desire. His eyes took in every inch of her body, darkening as they roamed over the smooth skin of her belly to the glossy pale curls trimming the wet, swollen petals of her sex. The body she was in was beautiful, but it was still Ella inside. And no man had ever gazed at her like that. Her thighs trembled as he lifted one graceful leg in his hands, caressing the calf.

"Don't be afraid. You're beautiful. Let me show you."

Ella nearly came off the bed when his mouth closed around her toes, treating each one to gentle lashes of his tongue. His lips gave the same careful treatment to her instep, and he licked at her ankle decadently when he reached it. Her breathy sighs stopped him.

"You like that, do you?"

She strained against the shirt that bound her as his mouth slowly traveled up the soft, warm flesh of her leg, past the knee to her inner thigh. Droplets of sweat trickled over her ribs toward her back as she writhed, the anticipation excruciating as his lips approached her most private place.

His breath fanned hot against the small patch of blonde curls and she shivered in desire. She watched in fascination as he lowered himself onto his elbows and wrapped his strong arms about her thighs, spreading them wider, mastering her.

"Do you want me to taste you, Elegant?" Ian asked, his face a mask of desire.

"Yes!"

His mouth lowered to her, pulling a low moan from her lips. His tongue slowly traced the seam of her outer lips before delving into the slick inner flesh that cried out for his touch. He teased the delicate flesh with quick flicks of his tongue, paying no heed to her thrashing or the fact she was mindless with pleasure. Ian held her in place and thoroughly tasted her, his tongue zeroing in on the small button where she wanted it most. He teased the tight, little bud with the tip of his tongue, bringing her to the edge of climax and then backing off to tease the surrounding flesh before she could come.

She didn't know how long he toyed with her before he finally began to nip and suck at her pleasure spot in earnest. He didn't stop when she dug her heels into the mattress and began to push herself at him as hard as she could. The touches of his tongue didn't stop with her screams or her begging for release. No, he held her open to his ministrations until, at last, she felt like her entire body was bursting, shattering. The room spun away as release finally overtook her.

Blinking as the room came back into view, Ella felt Ian moving toward her. She was dimly aware that he'd unfastened his jeans as she felt the vibrations still twitching low in her body, recovering from the most exquisite experience she'd ever known. She wanted to hold him, kiss him.

One look at the intensity of his gorgeous face told her that would have to wait. She caught a glimpse of him—long, thick and throbbing before his body lowered to hers. The passion of his kiss took her breath away and he entered her in a single smooth thrust a second later.

Ella's thighs closed about his slim hips as he began to glide smoothly in and out of her wetness. Her body stretched to accommodate him as he established an intoxicating rhythm within her, the rough denim of his jeans scraping her inner thighs with each thrust. How quickly the sensations began to build again as he took her, teasing her breasts, ears and shoulders with his playful tongue all the while. She could smell her own musk on him as he kissed her and played with her.

"God, you feel so good," Ian moaned as he continued to stroke himself in her, building her craving again while fighting his own release.

Ella gripped the shirt that restrained her, feeling her second release approaching, her pleasure intensified by his knowing eyes as he watched her. Her legs locked around his, holding him to her, never wanting him to stop.

"You're close aren't you?" he whispered.

She nodded.

Ian's hand slid between their bodies and his fingertips found her clit. Delicately, he toyed with the sensitive nub until she screamed when the next wave overtook her. It went on and on because he never stopped thrusting, never ceased the relentless push and drag of his pulsing flesh inside her. She felt boneless as he continued his movements; she felt his entire body tensing, the muscles rigid and unyielding.

His moans were loud as he finally allowed himself release. The long, hard shaft of his cock pulsed inside her and she felt his passion jetting into her again and again. Ian collapsed on top of her and she enjoyed his weight and the feeling of his damp flesh against her own.

Ian lifted himself up to release her hands, his blue eyes drowsy. Ella rubbed at her wrists only a little as she gazed up into this handsome face, happier than she could ever remember being.

"You're incredible, Elegant."

The warmth of his eyes had her heart skipping beats.

"Would you like to tell me now why you looked so sad back at the restaurant? And why you're wearing men's clothing? Are you running from someone?"

He had *noticed. Damn!*

"No, I'm not running away." She stuck with honesty. "The clothes belong to a friend of mine. He's gay. I borrowed them because—" Her mind scrambled for an excuse, but she'd always been a bad liar. "Well, yesterday I…"

"Answer me this," Ian picked up when she faltered. "Do you belong to someone else?"

"No, I'm not married."

"That's helpful." His grin came out again in all its glory. "But what about your heart?"

"There's no one."

"Good." His smile gentled as he kissed her slowly and gently. He rolled away to lie on his side, pulled her back against him and into the warmth of his body.

Ella enjoyed the way the thick hair on his thighs felt against the smooth flesh of her own.

Within moments, his breath slowed into the cadence of sleep and she joined him shortly after.

CHAPTER 4

True to his word, Ian had kept her from sleeping most of the night. Ella ached pleasantly in places she didn't know could ache the next morning as she pulled on the black shirt Ian had worn the day before and padded quietly into his kitchen. The soft fabric felt so good against her skin, and it smelled like him. Ella liked that.

She spotted the phone right off in the shiny, modern kitchen. But she'd call Richard later. She was starving.

Ella didn't expect to find much in the way of food in a bachelor's refrigerator or cabinets. But she was pleasantly surprised. He had a few basics—eggs, butter, bread. Bending to inspect the lower shelves of the refrigerator, she even spotted some cheese. *Perfect,* she thought, and got started on breakfast.

She'd thought to treat him to breakfast in bed, but he surprised her in the kitchen just as she transferred the omelets to the fine, gold-trimmed plates she'd found. How easily she could have dropped those plates as his large hands closed over her breasts and pulled her back against him. The hot ridge of his arousal rubbed suggestively against the top of her buttocks.

"That's quite a breakfast, Elegant," his voice purred into her ear.

Warmth seeped into her face at his praise. Ella had prepared two generous omelets, a neat stack of toast slices and another plate of French toast.

Flustered, she gently set the plates on the table and turned to smile up at him. "I thought you might be hungry."

His low growl startled her. "I am."

Swatting at the hands that pulled her hips against his, she shook her head. "For food."

With a dramatic sigh, he turned his attention to her culinary efforts and smiled. "I could have a bite. But that's a lot of food, Elegant."

"You need to keep up your strength." She surprised herself with that coy statement.

"Aye." The heat of his gaze had her taking a step back. "I do, don't I?"

To her relief, only because her stomach was growling, he took a seat at the table. His eyes never left her as she made a plate for him.

"I want to know more about you," he said.

Ella placed the plate in front of him and began to work on her own. "There's not much to tell."

"Where do you live?"

Ella panicked at the direction the conversation was headed. She nearly dropped her omelet as she struggled to maintain her composure.

"I live here in the city."

Some of the warmth left his expression. "Where in the city?"

"Not far from your restaurant." Why did she say that? She couldn't tell him where she lived. She wouldn't want him to find her after the spell ended. Ella's mind scrambled for a story. "I'm staying with a friend at the moment."

A black eyebrow rose in question. "The gay one?"

"Yes," she answered as she added a slice of toast to her plate and sat down across from him. Letting him think she was staying with Richard seemed safe enough. "I lost my job not too long ago and he's helping me out."

After a moment, Ian nodded, glancing down at the enormous plate of food meant for his breakfast. The dark shadow of his beard gave him a dark, dangerous look, as did the rich black waves of his rumpled hair. His upper body was magnificently naked, all tight male muscle. She sighed. *How would I ever be able to give him up?*

Well, she had nearly a month to enjoy him now, she reminded herself—if the spell held true. She watched as he dug into his breakfast. After a couple of bites, he stopped and smiled. Oh, what that smile did to her insides!

"You're a hell of a cook, Elegant."

"Glad you like it." She returned his smile.

And right then and there, she decided no matter what she *would* enjoy her month with him. Sure, he'd have questions. He was already asking things about her. Well, she wasn't about to say or do a thing to give him any idea that their time would come to an abrupt end in a month. If he knew, it would only ruin what they'd started. She'd simply disappear at the month's end. And since the spell conjured his attraction along with her temporary beauty, perhaps anything he felt for her would disappear when it ended.

The thought of that was too sad for her to consider at the moment.

"What are you thinking about?" His voice was a soft intrusion on her thoughts.

"I was thinking I'd like to go shopping today," Ella recovered nicely. Hell, she *had* to go shopping today. She'd never gone braless so long since puberty and she was still embarrassed about having been caught not wearing panties. Besides, she couldn't continue to borrow Richard's clothes. Once he spotted the spaghetti on his sweater, she was a goner!

"Shopping, huh?"

Ella only nodded because her mouth was full of omelet and toast. Alarmed, she realized she'd put away the omelet in record time. She swallowed hard.

"Nice to see a woman with a hearty appetite." He winked at her from the other side of the table. Then he laughed. "Sorry. Not something a woman wants to hear. All right then, let's talk about your shopping. What are you shopping for?"

"Clothes."

"I'll go with you," he threw out as he ate. "I might even pick up the tab if you buy a thing or two that I like."

She nearly choked on her toast. But before she protested, she thought better of it. *Why not? Wouldn't it be fun to try on things for him?* All the midriff-showing, hip hugging things she'd never been able to wear? She felt guilty he'd be spending money on her…

Remember, you are supposed to be enjoying yourself.

"What is going on in that head of yours?" Ian pushed his plate away and gazed at her. "You're a shy girl, Elegant. It's a nice change. But sometimes shy girls…think too much."

Ella stopped gnawing on her toast as he rose from his chair. Her nerve endings went on red alert as he closed in on her, turning the chair with her in it to face him before kneeling in front of her on the floor.

"I like an intelligent woman," he continued as if they were having a casual conversation. "Don't get me wrong. But there is time enough at night for dreaming. I like to live life right now."

And before she knew what he was about, he pushed her legs apart, captured her hips in his hands and took her with his mouth. The toast crumbled in her tight grip as his tongue traced the sensitive flesh between her thighs, and mercilessly teased the center of her pleasure. The soreness blended with the marvel of his lapping tongue sent her senses soaring. Clutching his hair, she held him to her as she writhed in the chair, helpless to do anything else.

Before she could reach climax, he stopped. His face split into a wide grin as her hands flew to the fastenings of his jeans. In an instant, she'd pushed them down his hips and wrapped her legs around his waist, guiding him towards her. Ian caught her easily in his arms and lowered her to the floor.

"Now that's what I was thinking." His voice was ragged with desire.

"You think too much," she gasped as he entered her in slow thrust.

Ian laughed as he began to move in her, gripping her hips to deepen his penetration. Ella's fingers dug into the carpeting, enjoying the way he filled her, possessed her.

He yanked the shirt up to her neck and moaned at the two tight points he found. His mouth closed around one then the other, laving them gently in turn, even as his hips maintained a solid, driving rhythm, in and out of her wet, hot channel. The sensations built quickly and, within moments, she lost control, clutching at him as waves of exquisite pleasure burst through her.

Ian didn't cease in his work. Relentlessly, he stroked himself into her body, his erection growing harder, pushing deeper, as he continued. He'd discovered the night before that it drove her crazy when he teased her shoulder with his tongue. Now when he did it, she nearly bucked him off she was so overcome with passion. He only chuckled as he held her in place, tracing wet circles on her shoulder as he continued to fuck her.

When she came the second time, he went with her, nearly crushing her in his embrace at the end.

"Ian?" Ella managed after a moment, breathless from his loving.

His breath came faster than hers. "Hmmm?"

"I think I've changed my mind about shopping today." She pushed a shiny, black lock of his hair away from his eyes. "I don't think I'll be able to walk."

Ian threw back his head and laughed. "Yes, you can."

* * *

And so went many days with Ian. Ella often wondered if the spell made him seem to be the perfect man or if he truly was. Being the co-owner of a restaurant, and various other businesses it turned out, he had to spend a certain amount of time at his office or in meetings. Aside from that, his time was devoted to her.

So many wonderful memories. Trying on clothes for Ian until he followed her into the shop's changing room and took her against the wall. He'd whispered in her ear that she couldn't cry out as he drove up into her. And exciting as that had been, it was nothing compared to the experience of watching him love her, watching them both in the fitting room mirror. If she hadn't felt everything so exquisitely, it would have been like watching a movie, watching Ian with a beautiful make-believe version of herself.

Then there was the night she'd cooked dinner for Ian and greeted him at the door wearing only his black leather jacket and a pair of black stiletto heels he'd bought for her. She could still hear the plates crashing to the floor after he'd swept them from the table, pressed her onto its surface and spread her beneath him. What a night of loving that had been!

But it hadn't all been about sex. There were other moments—tender moments. One night, she'd taken a long luxurious bath, a real treat since it wasn't something she normally felt comfortable with, and Ian had joined her in the tub. He'd told her funny tales of his childhood in Ireland, cradling her against his chest until the water had grown cold.

Another night, Ian had taken her out for dinner with his partners and their wives. He'd given her a single red rose that night, just before they'd entered the restaurant. He'd wrapped his arm possessively about her and introduced her with pride to his business partners and friends.

That's when she knew she'd fallen in love with him.

* * *

Perched on the edge of his bed, Ella glanced back over her shoulder and watched Ian lovingly as he slept. She'd only been back to her own apartment twice the entire month, though she talked to Richard on the phone nearly every day.

By tomorrow night, the full moon would be back and the spell would be broken. Ella fought the tears as she glanced down at the rose she'd pressed in a book. She'd done a good job of hiding her sadness from Ian as their time grew short. And she'd kept her promise to herself to enjoy every moment of being with him.

But there was one nagging fear that wouldn't let go.

She had her memories. But would it be enough?

At some point tomorrow, his Elegant would be gone and Ella Kent the Elephant would be back. But she found she didn't care about that at all. *Sure it's been an incredible thing to be beautiful for a month.* But the true gift she had drawn from that Gypsy's jar had been learning to accept herself. Once she'd been freed from her negative image of herself, and not worried one wit about her appearance or how other people saw her, she'd enjoyed life so much. The freedom she felt had been incredible. And she knew it was the one thing, aside from her memories, that she'd take with her. It wouldn't be as easy to feel that way when she went back to normal, she knew, but she vowed never to go back to being so down on herself again.

She was losing something, too. Her heart. It would go with Ian.

With a weary sigh, she returned the book to the bedside table.

"Come here." His voice was scratchy from sleep as he reached for her in the dark. He pulled her against him, cradling her against his chest as he slept. For Ella, it was the best place in the world to be.

And then she finally let the tears come. Once he left for work tomorrow morning, she'd never see him again.

CHAPTER 5

Seven months later

"I got quite a deal on these ornaments at the florist shop," Richard announced as he walked into her living room.

Ella rose from the floor where she'd been decorating the bottom of her Christmas tree, smoothing the skirt of her new red dress as she stood.

"Oh, yeah?"

"Wow," Richard said as his gaze moved over her.

Ella grinned at him. "You like it?"

Richard motioned for her turn around and she did. The incredulous look was still on his face when she again faced him.

"What?"

"Ella, you look great," he finally said. "I guess I couldn't tell how much weight you'd lost when you wore your old clothes but you look…wonderful."

"It's a size ten," she announced proudly. She had to admit she was still quite the full-figured gal, but nonetheless she was pleased with her appearance. She'd grown her hair out, she'd shed nearly one hundred and forty pounds, and had even joined the gym that Richard went to.

Buying new clothes had been fun and melancholy all at the same time. How wonderful it had been to do something for herself, to boost her confidence with smaller, stylish clothes. She'd hardly been able to believe it herself when she'd gotten into the dress she now wore.

Still, she couldn't go near a fitting room without thinking of Ian.

It had been seven months since that morning she'd left him, and not a day went by when she didn't wonder what he was doing, and if he ever thought of her. He'd called once that first week, but since the initial of her first name, Mary, was on her phone listing, she lied and told him he had the wrong number. He still called Richard every now and then to see if he'd had any word from her. Richard always pled ignorance because she'd made him.

As if he could read her thoughts, Richard said, "You should call him."

"We've talked about this." She feigned annoyance, mostly because she didn't want him to see how very badly she wanted to take his advice. "That's not a good idea."

"Why? I could understand if you still looked…were…like you used to." Richard struggled. "But now? You don't look all that different from when you drank the potion. You—"

"Please!" she cut him off. "I look a *lot* different from that and you know it."

"Ella, I swear, now you've lost the weight, all you'd need to do is get collagen injections for your lips and you'd be right back!"

Ella tried her hardest to glare at him. "Richard, you're a good friend, but you and I both know that's not true."

Shaking his head at her, he continued, "So, do you have to look exactly like that? I don't think so. After all the times you've made me talk to him, I think I know how he feels about you. He wouldn't care, El."

Her heart pounded out a hopeful rhythm at his words, but her rational side pushed her hopes back down.

"Even if I do look similar to that now, Richard, how would I ever be able to explain why I left him? Well, without him thinking I'm crazy."

"You could think of something." After an awkward moment, Richard handed her the shopping bag he still held. "Here are the ornaments. And I'm off. I'm having a couple of the cellists over for dinner."

Ella smiled at her friend. "Any prospects?" she teased.

"Both." He winked at her. "Tall, dark and handsome."

Instantly, an image of Ian filled her mind. "Sounds great."

"How's the new job?"

"Good," Ella admitted. And it was.

Not long after her time with Ian ended, she found a nice job in an Italian restaurant. It was a little farther away, but much nicer than the café where she used to work, and the tips had been excellent. That she'd been able to avoid the rich Italian food, her favorite, to accomplish what she did had been nothing short of miraculous.

In the last two weeks, Ella had been promoted to hostess and she loved the chance to do something different. And when she wasn't hostess, she helped with bookkeeping responsibilities. Things couldn't be better.

"Have a good time." She waved her friend on.

No sooner had Richard closed the door than she peered into the bag of ornaments he'd brought her and she noticed something. A sleek bottle of wine nestled at the bottom of the bag.

Well, he'll be wanting that, she thought and headed out the door towards his apartment to return it to him. She'd just turned the corner when she encountered a tall, familiar figure knocking on his door ahead of her. Shock rooted her to the spot as Ian glanced her way. Those blue eyes that had haunted her dreams lit up with recognition.

"Ella?"

Richard casually opened the door, clearly expecting his guests. Her friend's eyes rounded in surprise at the scene that greeted him.

Ian didn't seem to notice when Richard reached for the wine bottle Ella held out to him and closed the door again.

"Aren't you going to speak to me?" Ian prompted.

Ella began trembling fiercely. She was so happy to see him. His shiny black hair was a little longer than she remembered, he looked a tiny bit thinner, but every bit as handsome in his long, black coat with a dark gray scarf the same shade as his trousers. She wanted to run to him, to tell him—

Tell him what?

"Hello, Ian." She fought the tremor in her voice. "How have you been?"

His blue eyes were angry slits as he approached her.

"How am I?" Ian towered over her in the shadowy hallway. "How am I? How the hell do you think I am? I've been looking for you for months, Ella. You just took off. No note, no warning. You've never called."

"Ian, I'm sorry," she said and meant it. "I didn't want to leave you. I—"

And that's when she noticed that the left sleeve of his coat hung empty from the elbow down, where his arm should have been. "Ian? What happened?"

An emotion she couldn't name crossed his features. "Is there somewhere we can talk?"

"My apartment is down the hall." No harm in telling him now.

She closed the door behind him, crushed by guilt that he'd come to harm since she'd left. Ella found his gaze roaming over her and she felt uncomfortable under his scrutiny. Did he still find her attractive? Did she look anywhere close to what he remembered?

"Ella, you look different."

"Heavier." She jumped in before he could say something else.

"Better." A hint of that devilish smile came out. "I like a woman with a little meat on her bones. Didn't want to say anything before, but you were so damned skinny."

Ella laughed. She couldn't help it. Inside her chest, her heart bloomed with hope. Maybe he could accept her after all. Maybe he could love her…

But the sadness returned to his gaze as he motioned toward his missing arm. "I've something to explain to you. And it's not going to be easy."

"Your arm." Ella took a cautious step forward. "What happened, Ian?"

"Ella, I lost my arm in a car accident twenty years ago," he said flatly. "When I was fifteen."

It took a moment for his words to sink in, to jar her out of her guilt. "Fifteen?"

"Ella, it's hard to be…disabled. To have everyone eye you with pity, look at you like you're something different." His blue eyes locked with hers. "Most days, you'd give anything for a break from it all, no matter how short."

Her heart pounded as suspicion crept into her mind. *Could it be?* "Even if it is only for a month?"

Ian nodded first. Then his eyes narrowed on her. "Why did you say that?"

The jar was on her mantle along with her other favorite things. She could feel his eyes on it before she picked it up.

Before she could turn around, he asked, "Where did you get that?"

Ella smiled at his surprised expression. "From a Gypsy woman at Navy Pier," she explained. "I bought it on my thirtieth birthday. It was to make me beautiful for a month. And it did. I weighed over two hundred pounds before I drank it, Ian."

Ian shook his head in disbelief.

"Ian, you saw me! You knocked me over in the restaurant the night I drank it." She met his gaze squarely, willing him to believe her. "Don't you remember knocking down an enormous blonde woman around that time?"

His mouth dropped open. "My God."

"You drank it, too, didn't you? And for a month you had your arm back."

He nodded. "I took the witch's brew the day we met."

So that's why he didn't look at her with pity that night, she realized. He knew what it was like.

"But I don't understand something." Ian's gaze raked over her. "Did you take it again? You look...well, a wee bit heavier. But you look nothing like the night I ran you over."

Ella blushed and he smiled.

"In the time I was with you, I came to realize I'd spent much of my life worrying about what people thought of me. I didn't want to live like that any more because of my weight."

"Ella, you don't look all that different from how you did the month we were together. Don't you see?

"No," she said honestly. "But I am happy with myself now."

"Are you happy with your life then, Ella?"

Her heart nearly skipped a beat at the longing in his gaze. "No...because I've missed you."

Ian reached her in a second and the jar went crashing to the floor as he captured her with his arm, the arm that had lifted her in the restaurant, and kissed her until she was breathless. The taste of him, the feel of him, was heaven to her.

When he pulled back from her, his expression was serious. His gaze shifted to his ruined arm and back. "Ella, there's nothing I can do about this. There are prosthetics, but I just wanted to be like everyone else again, even for a little while. I didn't plan on meeting a beautiful woman, but since I did, I damn well enjoyed it. And then I couldn't forget about her. I fell in love with her."

Ella pulled his mouth to hers and poured every bit of love and passion she felt for him into it. Ian loved her. He accepted her. And that was all that mattered. Deliberately, she clutched his ruined arm, running her hand down to where it ended abruptly in the long woolen sleeve. That his arm was missing didn't matter at all.

"I love you, Ian," she whispered. "Just as you are."

"Ella, that's easy to say but—"

"You require proof then?"

The caution in Ian's eyes began to fade at her suggestive smile. "I'd like proof, Elegant."

Pulling his body to hers, she burrowed into his coat and rubbed herself against him. The hot bulge that pressed to her belly made her shiver in anticipation.

"Let's go."

Ella, happier than she could ever remember being, led Ian off to her bedroom. The broken shards of the broken Gypsy's jar vanished the moment the door closed.

WOMAN IN CHAINS

CHAPTER 1

The Loire Valley France, 1816

"*Cette fille est jolie.*"

Mia Emmerson knew the word "*jolie*." The French word for "pretty" or "beautiful." Unfortunately, there weren't very many other words in the language that she understood. She struggled to translate the rest of the sentence as thick fingers lifted her chin.

Madame d'Entremont's gray eyes were sharp and assessing. The leering scrutiny of the large, garishly dressed woman made Mia uneasy. Her full, over-ripe body seemed ready to burst from the revealing scarlet gown that she wore. A dark shade of red that reminded Mia of blood, stained the woman's lips and cheeks, accentuated by the dramatic upsweep of her sable hair. And Mia had never seen jewels as fine as the impressive spray of rubies and diamonds glittering across the creamy expanse of the woman's cleavage.

She turned Mia's head to afford a view of each side of her face, evaluating her as if she were a bauble being considered for purchase. Mia thought of pulling away, but the gray eyes moving over her flashed a warning. The woman's warm fingers caressed her jaw covetously before falling away and a wave of apprehension swept over Mia.

"Edward?" Mia swallowed nervously, looking to him for an explanation.

"Quiet!" Edward Cross hissed, running a pudgy hand through his thinning black hair. His eyes were the same shade of black, and were hard and mean as they bored into her.

The woman stepped closer until her enormous breasts pressed against Mia's arm and the heavy musk of her perfume enveloped them both. Before Mia knew what was happening, the woman's hands boldly began to move over her body, squeezing her breasts, her backside. One hand slid down to cup her through the thin muslin skirt of her dress, fingers probing through the fabric and between her thighs. Gasping in shock, Mia yanked away.

Madame d'Entremont laughed at the flush of humiliation that warmed her face. "*Elle est plutôt gênée.*"

"What are you saying?" Mia asked, trying to keep the fear from her voice.

The woman looked to Edward before returning her sardonic gaze to Mia. "You do not speak French?" she asked, her English heavily accented.

Mia lifted her chin a notch. "No, I do not," she replied tersely.

With her heart thundering in fear, Mia stared at Edward, damning him for the nightmare turn her life had taken since her father's death the year before. Within a fortnight of her sire's passing, Edward had arrived at their home in Cornwall and proclaimed himself the impoverished baron's heir. There'd been no one to stop him. Her father, who'd always enjoyed good health, had never had a will prepared and the fever to which he had swiftly succumbed had left no time to see it done. It had been all too easy for his nephew, Edward Cross, Earl of Lester, with his vast fortune and immense arrogance, to lay claim to all that had belonged to her father. Specifically his land.

Unfortunately that included her, too. Edward was her guardian now and in control of her future. That was the taunt he constantly threw at her anyway.

"No matter," Madame d'Entremont continued with a dismissing wave of her hand. "My clientele will not care if you speak at all. *Oui,* some of them would prefer that, *ma belle anglaise.*"

Mia's mind reeled in confusion. "Your clientele?"

Edward shot her a hostile glare. His velvety tone, however, held only a thread of warning. "You have been unhappy in my care, Mia. It has been quite obvious to me since I arrived at your door to save you from being tossed out into the streets. You've been exceedingly unpleasant when you should have been damned grateful to have someone like myself looking after your welfare."

Only fear kept her from laughing. Unpleasant was she? What had he expected? That she would be grateful for the way he'd swept into her life and lied to her, stolen from her?

Taking a menacing step toward her as if he thought she might flee, his short, bulky body tensed. "I told you that I controlled your future, didn't I? I have arranged for you to reside with Madame d'Entremont. She manages a very successful business. You will work for her."

"Work for her?" Mia realized a shiver of panic. "But I couldn't—"

"You will develop the skills I require in time, *ma joli.*" Madame d'Entremont leaned forward and lowered her voice. "And you will learn them well."

Mia felt sick as the realization of what was to happen to her sank in. The woman wanted her to work as a courtesan. She began to tremble as she recalled the scantily clad women they had passed on their way to the office. Why had she not been more suspicious of her cousin's motives? The unexpected journey to France, his unusually pleasant mood of late. The mysterious events of the last several weeks began to make sense.

At least she had managed to get a note out to Adam Wood before they had left, so someone would know where she was. Adam would try to help her, would know something wasn't right. The young, gentle viscount was her friend.

But until he came to look for her she would be at the mercy of the lewd woman standing before her and the countless men who frequented her establishment. Mia had only the faintest idea of what privately transpired between a man and a woman. And she couldn't speak French well at all. That would only serve to make things worse. The thought that she would give herself freely to strange men for money made her stomach clench.

Mia could barely speak. "Why?"

But she knew the answer. She had caught the eye of Edward's French lover, Philippe. Her cousin's vulgar paramour made no secret of the fact that he enjoyed men and women equally, though what that specifically entailed she wasn't certain. She did understand the advances Philippe had made toward her in the last few weeks. So did Edward. Understanding heightened the sickness she already felt. Her cousin wanted to punish her for being his unwitting rival.

Edward's lips thinned in anger. "What else am I to do with you, cousin? My dear uncle, your father, left me very little money and a pitifully neglected residence. Did the old fool think I would devotedly care for you out of the goodness in my heart?"

"My father didn't leave you anything," Mia said with heavy bitterness. "You took what you wanted."

His thin lips curled into a snarl. "It's mine," he growled.

He had what he wanted. And he definitely wanted to rid himself of *her*. The thought gave her a moment of hope.

"Let me go." Mia hated herself for pleading yet it was her only chance. "Please, you have Gavin Hall, the money. You will never see me again. I swear it."

His brows shot up in surprise. "Why would I allow that to happen when Madame d'Entremont has offered me such a handsome sum for you?"

The woman's amused smile confirmed his words. "You are a virgin, *oui*?"

Coloring fiercely, Mia glared at her cousin. "You bastard," she said in a choked voice.

She held her head high as she watched his eyes darken with fury, his face redden with rage. He drew back a large hand to strike her.

"*Non!* Not her face!" The woman rushed forward to prevent the blow. "This."

A stunning punch to the stomach rewarded Mia for her efforts, the blow nearly bringing her to her knees. The woman's meaty fist hovered before her face, threatening more. Mia didn't move.

"You have spirit, *ma jolie*." The woman bent to whisper in her ear. "It will not serve you here. You understand, *oui*?"

Mia fought a wave of nausea. "Yes," she croaked.

"We have an agreement then?" she heard Edward ask as the woman released her.

"*Oui*." Madame d'Entremont's voice was cold and exact. "She pleases me."

Mia managed to glance up in time to see the madam opening the parlor door, signaling to someone beyond it. When she turned back, her eyes focused on Mia. "Her virtue will no doubt earn me a small fortune, but her face and her tight little body..." The woman's face lit up with evil glee. "She will be most popular."

Two young men in matching uniforms entered the room, heading for Mia. Panic rioted within her as they each grasped one of her arms.

"Edward," she begged, looking to her cousin as she struggled against her captors. "Please, don't do this."

Edward watched the scene with a look of undisguised satisfaction as she was pulled from the room.

CHAPTER 2

"Thank you, my lords, for whatever you can do," Adam Wood's high voice pleaded. The willowy youth could be no more than twenty, Anthony guessed. He looked much younger.

Anthony Montford, the fourth Duke of Ashton, scowled at his friend as the young viscount left his study. "You think me so bored in exile that I will jump to do that whelp's bidding? I don't care how much bloody money he offers."

"So you plan to spend the entire winter feeling sorry for yourself? Or do you plan to break the monotony now and again by drinking yourself into a stupor?"

"I am indulging in neither self-pity nor drink. Is it so difficult to understand that I simply desire to live in solitude?"

"Liar," Nicholas accused as Anthony drained his glass.

Nicholas Wolfe, Viscount of Carlingford, shook his head. Leaning back in the wing chair across from Anthony, he stared at the half-empty brandy snifter he held as if in deep thought. "Well, you might have told me earlier of this great need for solitude." He placed ugly emphasis on *solitude*. "And spared yourself my tedious company."

Anthony almost smiled at his friend's half attempt to make him feel guilty. Refilling his glass with the fine brandy he'd been enjoying since early evening, he sighed. He knew where Nick was going with this and he wasn't certain he could stomach the lecture again. He felt no regret for the way he lived his life. He didn't owe anyone a damned thing. All he wanted was to be left alone. Nick had been his closest friend since childhood and perhaps his only friend now. And while he grudgingly admitted to enjoying his friend's occasional visits, he could live without them.

"Don't, Nick," he warned.

The threat in his tone would have humbled any other man. Anthony knew from the few visits he had made to the nearby town that the rumors had followed him to France. The townsfolk were careful to keep their distance, regarding him as they would the devil himself. Even his servants moved warily about him, criminals and whores themselves, scrambling to do his bidding and ready to flee at the first sign of displeasure.

Unimpressed, Nick smirked at him from his chair. He knew Anthony better than anyone, knew he had nothing to fear. As if reading his thoughts, Nick said, "It has been three years since the trials and Julianna's death, Tony. You—"

"Save your speech tonight." Anthony's tone was icy. "It bores me."

"Ah." His friend took another sip of brandy, his eyes sparkling with amusement. "So you are bored with me, too. You are hard on one's ego, old man."

Anthony fought the urge to throttle him. While he was certain he could pound his friend into leaving him in peace, he was in no mood for the pummeling that he would have to endure in order to do it. Nicholas was damned near his equal in size and strength and loved a good fight.

Frustrated, he raked a hand through his hair. "Go to hell," he growled.

Nick chuckled dryly. "You'd like that, wouldn't you?"

"At the moment, yes."

"I have a better idea," Nick offered, leaning forward. A lock of raven hair fell over his forehead. Absently, he tugged at his cravat as if it were too tight.

Anthony stared at him. "No. I'm not wasting my time on that boy."

"Yes, you will." Nicholas' face split into a wide grin. "That boy has a bloody fortune at his disposal." Nick's broad shoulders blocked Anthony's view of the fire as he spread his arms wide in an extravagant gesture. "All you have to do is fetch his poor maiden, ensure that her pederast guardian never troubles her again and you'll have enough coin to return to your pirating if that is your wish."

The proposition did hold some appeal. When Anthony had fled England three years before, a convicted pirate and murderer, he'd been able to take very little of his wealth with him. The country chateau where he currently resided was the only holding left in his possession, his coffers ever dwindling. The money the viscount offered for so simple a task would offer him freedom. To return to the sea, to do whatever he desired. And Nick was probably right. Perhaps such an evening of revelry would make him feel better. He'd missed those days from his youth when such evenings were common and he'd been so carefree…

Slowly, Anthony shook his head. Years ago he would have accepted his friend's invitation. But fate and time had made him a different man. Guilt over the death of a woman who'd loved him had made him a different man. No longer did he view the world as an endless well he could draw pleasure from. Now he saw only a sea of faces filled with fear and loathing.

"No, I don't think so." Anthony used a cool tone to give the impression of indifference.

But Nick played at not hearing that. And he did it badly. "I wonder why the girl means so much to him that he would offer such a sum for her rescue?"

"Probably didn't have the chance to rut between her legs before she was snatched away." Anthony eyed his friend, curious. "Why are you so interested? You've no plan to be involved."

"I'm not a known criminal," Nick winked at him. "You are. But that aside, I remember how much you once craved adventure. He's offering money, which you need, adventure, which you used to enjoy. And it is all taking place right here under your nose, in the village. All you have to do is take the girl back and you'll have enough money to do whatever you want. It will get you out of this damnable place and out of your cups anyway."

Setting his snifter aside, Nicholas slowly rose from his chair, straightening his navy blue coat. He'd neatly trapped Anthony and he knew it. "Just think about it, Anthony. But don't take too long. Dear Mia is waiting."

With a knowing smile, Nicholas gave him a quick wink before quitting the room.

Well, hell.

CHAPTER 3

Anthony smiled as he accepted a snifter of brandy from Madame d'Entremont and settled back into the chair she offered him, relaxed. It had been surprising to learn that the girl had been delivered to such a notorious brothel. The house was known far and wide throughout France for offering the most decadent delights of every kind.

And since business had brought Anthony here…well, why not enjoy it? If the house wench he'd just enjoyed or any of the other staff members knew his identity, they said nothing. It was all about money, he knew. As long as he had the coin, they wouldn't say a word. And he had a nice bag of coins from his young patron.

The madam took a seat across from him, her painted mouth curving into a smile. "You wished to see me, my lord?" Her tone was edged with concern. "Was Cosette not to your liking?"

Releasing a sigh of satisfaction, Anthony returned her smile. The buxom blonde could do incredible things with her hands and mouth. "I assure you, Madame, she was very much to my liking."

"Then how may I help you?" she asked.

Anthony appreciated her direct approach. "You are known for being able to grant most any wish your clients have. Mine is simple. While the women of France are beautiful and…talented, I find myself homesick for an English rose. I don't suppose you have such a flower in your garden."

Her grin widened wickedly. "You are a virile man, no?"

"Indeed," he took a sip of the fine brandy.

Madame d'Entremont's gray eyes gleamed with interest. "I do have such a rose in my garden. But the girl is fresh. A virgin. I have set a high price for the privilege of being first to sample her charms."

Anthony frowned. "I think you place too much value on innocence. Do the majority of your clients really find it so appealing?"

The woman eyed him speculatively.

"If not, they would still find this girl to be irresistible. She is a rare beauty."

"But inexperienced," he pointed out.

"If you seek to bargain with me about the sum I demand for this rose, our meeting is over." Her face became a mask of implacable calm. "Besides, you are hardly in a position to ask for concessions."

Anthony's fingers tightened around the fine crystal.

"I know who you are." Her eyes met his squarely. "Why should I allow such a dangerous man to pluck my rose?"

Biting back the nasty retort that immediately came to his tongue, he said only, "Because I will pay your price. I'm sure that you are anxious to see a profit from your investment."

It was a risk, he knew, to subtly point out that she bought and sold young women like cattle. Ah hell, it was the truth. And unless he missed his guess she'd paid a substantial amount for the girl he came for. But if the madam were offended, she took pains to hide it.

"Very well, my lord," she finally said. "Let us make arrangements. I will demand payment in advance."

"Agreed," he said easily. It wasn't his money after all.

"And…I wish to watch."

That caught him off guard. He felt the sting of resentment once the surprise faded.

"At least for a while," she added quickly.

"You fear I will harm her?" His tone turned menacing. "Did I hurt your other wench?"

That she was apprehensive was plain enough in her expression. But there was something else. He watched the woman absently smooth her hair. Her smile was small, secretive.

"Or is that you are very fond of your rose?" Anthony suggested, receiving his answer in the interested gleam of her eyes. So she wanted the girl herself. It piqued his curiosity.

It would complicate matters greatly to go along with her wish. But what choice did he really have?

"Watch then."

He fished the bag of coins from his coat and tossed them into her lap.

"Shall we adjourn to my garden, my lord?" The madam's response was eager.

It was done then. She would take him to the girl. Pleased with himself, Anthony drained his glass, enjoying the feeling of the brandy burning its way towards his stomach.

"Yes, let's adjourn."

CHAPTER 4

Mia shivered before the roaring blaze in the fireplace, its warmth unable to soothe her shaking limbs. Her stomach clenched tight as she glanced about the room behind her.

The huge, four poster bed was the centerpiece of the room done up in shades of dark red and gold. Soft light reflected off the shiny surface of the counterpane, glittered off the golden threads woven into the draperies. The intricate pattern of the carpet beneath her knees matched perfectly the rich perfection of her surroundings.

Mia had hoped her newness would buy her some time to plan an escape. She hadn't been prepared for the fact that she might be entertaining a gentleman her first night.

The sound of heavy footsteps echoed beyond the door and she fought to keep her fragile control. She wanted to run as fast as her feet would carry her but it would only go worse for her, she knew, if she attempted unsuccessfully to escape. As if anticipating that she would try, the madam had posted guards outside her door and one several feet below the room's single window.

Please don't let him be an ogre, she prayed, her heart racing as the footsteps stopped outside the door. At least she had hoped he would be kinder than the hard faced retainers that the madam employed. Slowly, Mia turned her back to the door and faced the fire from her place on the floor.

The door opened soundlessly. Mia did not know he had entered the room until she heard the door close. She bowed her head, hiding her face behind a curtain of dark hair. Underneath her own heavy cloak, she trembled violently. *Please let this be over soon.*

The sound of footsteps resumed, lighter now. Mia shuddered as she felt him standing over her, chilled by his shadow.

"Are you trying to hide, little rose?"

Mia closed her eyes. He was an Englishman, his voice deep and velvety smooth. Anxiety pulsed through her as she felt him kneel next to her. His breath was warm in her hair.

"Let me see your face."

The soft caress of his voice sent an involuntary chill down her spine. Strong fingers cupped her chin and slowly turned her face.

His face was only inches from hers, his expression stilled and serious. While Mia had prepared herself for all sorts of monstrosities, nothing could have prepared her for the man before her. His face was boldly handsome with firm, sensual lips. The flickering light of the flames reflected off the tawny waves of his hair, dancing wickedly over the bronze of his skin. The eyes that studied her were shades of amber and gold, and held a glint of wonder.

Slowly, he rose from the floor, his powerful well-muscled body moving with ease. His white, linen shirt hung open to the broad expanse of his chest. Sleek black breeches smoothed over his slim hips and long legs. The large hand that had held her face extended to her. Mia hesitated, glancing up at him as a tumble of confused thoughts assailed her. In all her wild imaginings the last several hours, this possibility had never entered her mind. Never had she seen a man so strikingly attractive.

Absently, she placed her small hand in his. All too late she remembered the golden manacles around her wrists and the chain she wore beneath the heavy cloak.

Lifting the lightweight chain in his other hand, he stared. His golden eyes met hers but Mia tore her gaze away from his and stared at the rug at her feet. Preparing herself for the humiliation that would follow, she tried to focus her thoughts on her home in Cornwall, on anything but the man standing before her.

With agility she wouldn't have expected in such a large man, he grasped the hem of her cloak and eased the folds over her shoulders to reveal the indecent costume she wore.

Mia trembled and forced her arms to remain at her sides. She felt warmth flooding her face as she stood before him in the thin, revealing layers of fabric. Dressed as a slave girl, only her breasts and lower body were covered by solid panels of shining gold, while her arms and legs were wrapped in diaphanous layers, hiding little. The small bodice of the costume scooped low revealing the tops of her breasts and ending just beneath them, leaving her waist and the tender flesh of her belly completely uncovered. No one had ever seen her so exposed. She wanted to pull the cloak around her body once more, shrink into its depths.

His eyes darkened as they seductively moved over her. He used the costume chain to pull her closer, his scent a pleasant blend of sandalwood and brandy. His fingertips grazed her cheek, his touch almost unbearable in its tenderness.

"She pleases you, *oui*?"

A muscle at his firm jaw twitched and some dark emotion crossed his features for a fleeting moment.

He smiled at Mia then, a flash of straight white teeth smoothing out the cleft of his firm chin. He was incredibly handsome when he smiled.

"Indeed she does," he replied, his gaze never leaving Mia.

Why was Madame d'Entremont there? Surely she didn't mean to remain.

But apparently she did. Mia glanced helplessly from the smiling woman, who took a seat in a chair by the bed, back to him as his hand found her nape, disappearing under the spill of her long dark, hair. He towered over her, more than a head taller than she. She almost welcomed the strong arm that slid around her beneath the cloak, offering her support. She didn't know how much longer she could rely on her shaking knees to hold her up. A torrent of emotions, not the least of which his disturbing nearness, threatened to consume her. Unfamiliar warmth clashed with anxiety as it spread through her body. His fingers teased the flesh at the small of her back as his lips lowered to hers.

He took her mouth with tantalizing intensity, his lips caressing hers softly. Her heart jolted as he crushed her against him, his tongue tracing the seam of her lips. Despite her fear and the lewd woman watching them, her traitorous body began to relax against his long, hard form. Her submission only encouraged him as he pressed her tightly against him with the hand at her back. The hard ridge of his arousal moved provocatively against her naked belly.

Coaxing her lips apart, his tongue began a slow exploration of her mouth. Mia froze, fear reclaiming her. This was beyond her experience. Dear God, heat and chill assaulted her body like fever.

Feeling her tremors, his head lifted. Amber eyes studied her intently. His gaze moved down her body, stopping at the exposed skin covering her ribs. Mia knew he had spotted the ugly, purple bruise from the madam's blow, the powder applied by the girls who had dressed her a futile effort.

For a moment his expression was grim, dark. But just as quickly, his seductive smile was back. His hand slid up over her ribs, slowly over her breast to the clasp of her cloak. Mia shivered again as it fell to the floor.

"Let us make you more comfortable," he whispered, grabbing the golden chain and pulling her toward the bed. When Mia resisted, he yanked the chain sharply and sent her sprawling across the huge bed.

"Ah, ah, my lord." Madame d'Entremont's voice penetrated the veil of fear around her. "You must be careful with my rose."

"As you have been?" There was a thread of menace in his tone.

Mia tried to scramble away from him on the bed, but he caught her easily, looping the chain that linked her wrists over a thick hook in the wall, obviously intended for that purpose. Her heart pounded in her chest as he pulled her flat on the bed, her arms stretched over her head. A large hand slid over the flat plane of her stomach to cup her breast and she turned her head toward the small table by the bed and the curiously shaped glass objects placed on it. But no matter what she tried to focus on, think about, her body wouldn't let her ignore the sensations his fingers were creating as they slid into the bodice of her costume. Rough fingertips delicately teased her nipple as he lowered his body to hers.

She jumped when the warm wetness of his mouth found the slim column of her throat. His lips caressed the soft flesh below her lobe, then his tongue traced the outer shell of her ear. Mia twisted beneath him, pointless she knew, her actions only bringing his weight more firmly upon her. The unyielding hardness of his thigh pressed between her own, applying gentle pressure and causing an unfamiliar ache to build in her core.

What was wrong with her? While her heart raced in fear and her mind fought to shut out what was happening to her, her body had a will of its own. His hands on her flesh, his body pressed to hers, inspired a hunger she'd never encountered. The realization brought her to shame as his fingers pulled back the bodice to reveal her full white breast.

Mia's eyes flew back to him and she nearly came off the bed when his mouth closed over her nipple and his tongue teased the tip with gentle lashes. His thigh pressed against her center in a ceaseless rhythm as his mouth laved and caressed her. The sensations building within her nearly took her breath away. Propriety demanded she resist him, with her mind at least, since she could not physically, but in the silence, her body grew taut under the gentle torment.

A rustle of silk pulled her back to reality and the madam, all but forgotten, to Mia's shame, moved to sit by her on the other side of the bed. The man who held her captive seemed not to notice or care that the madam watched them with gleaming gray eyes. His mouth never ceased as it moved to suckle the other breast he had bared, and the heat of his loins relentlessly continued to nudge against her. The madam's hand slid across the coverlet to caress Mia's thigh at the same moment one of his hands slid down her body, his fingers gliding into her most private place to cup her through the thin fabric.

"Please," Mia begged, fear replacing incredible sensation as Madame d'Entremont edged closer to her. The woman's hand traveled up her body like a loathsome insect, her fingers finding the flesh of her breast, still damp from the man's ministrations.

The man's lips trailed up from her other breast to return to her ear. "Just another moment more," he whispered.

Mia had no idea what he meant and no time to consider it. The madam's mouth closed over her breast, wiping her mind clean of anything save shock. She'd barely recovered when the man's weight lifted from her.

His fist connected with the madam's nose, knocking her back off the bed. He was on her before she could cry out to the guards. Mia could see his arm draw back before delivering another solid blow to the woman on the floor. There was blood on his hand when he returned to the bed. Mia jumped in fright as he worked to release the chain from the hook above her head.

"Did you kill her?" Mia asked before she could stop herself.

"No." He hauled up the bodice of her costume to cover her breasts the moment he'd freed the chain. "I broke her nose. She will not be happy when she comes to."

He pulled Mia from the bed, bent to snatch her discarded cloak from the floor and hastily wrapped it about her, his large fingers shaking as he wrestled with the clasp.

"We are leaving," he said in a tone that would brook no argument. "I'm going to lower you out the window."

"But there is a guard down there," she pointed out as she fought to bring her trembling body under control.

He pulled her to the window and clasped her jaw in his large hand, forcing her gaze to meet his.

"I know. And that is no short distance to the ground. He will be forced to catch you. Do you understand?" He continued at her nod. "He'll have little time to act when I come down after you. When he drops you, run. Run toward the garden gate. One of my servants will await you there."

Mia shrugged out of his touch and took a step toward the window, relief that she would at least escape the madam's establishment washing over her. She couldn't deny she wanted to escape this man as well, for she feared the things he had made her feel, feared *him*.

As if he could read her thoughts, his hand caught her jaw again. The pad of his thumb gently skimmed across her cheek. Mia didn't miss the fact that his hand trembled. The intensity in his golden eyes mesmerized her.

Just as suddenly, his hand dropped and he motioned toward the window. "We haven't much time."

And with that he flung open the window and helped Mia to climb out.

CHAPTER 5

The one small window of the room Anthony had secured for them looked out over the poorest part of the village. The inn with its coarse wooden walls and dingy atmosphere housed whores and cutthroats nightly, their ribald laughter echoing up the stairs. It was the safest place for them to be. By now the madam's men would be looking for him at the chateau and, not finding him there, would expect that he would flee the valley.

Anthony seethed with mounting anger as he stared out the window into the winter night. It was well past midnight and he could barely make out the dim outline of the landscape beyond. It didn't matter. In truth, he stood before the window enjoying the pocket of cool air surrounding it, willing the throbbing in his loins to recede.

Damn Nicholas. He would throttle his friend the next time he saw him. It was high time his friend learned the consequences of interfering in his life. Anthony had made his wishes quite clear; he wanted solitude. His jaw clenched as he recalled numerous times he'd tried to explain his need to Nicholas.

Nicholas would have a good laugh at his expense if he could see him now. Hard as stone and alone with the beautiful object of his lust.

He turned to where she sat in the room's single chair, wrapped in the heavy dark cloak from neck to knee, only the slim lines of her ankles and the little gold slippers she wore revealed to him. She didn't move. Her head bowed so that she was hiding beneath a sleek curtain of dark hair. He wanted to see her face, needed to prove to himself that the brandy he'd consumed earlier had temporarily made her into the lovely creature of fantasy he'd held and kissed earlier. His hands shook at his sides. If he touched her, he feared what he might do.

"Look at me," Anthony said quietly, aware of the tremor in his voice.

Slowly lifting her head, she peered up at him. Anthony's breath caught. He stared in astonishment at the perfect, delicate features of her face. The smooth ivory of her skin was flawless. Her cheekbones were high and exotic, her rosy lips full. Her large, moss-green eyes were arresting, fringed with thick dark lashes. Gleaming, dark hair the color of chocolate fell in graceful curves over her shoulders.

He couldn't tear his gaze away from her. No amount of spirits could have produced such beauty. Gazing at her closely, he realized that she was even lovelier than he had imagined.

Slowly, his gaze slid downward over her slight form wrapped in the simple cloak. He'd thought having her fully covered would allow him to talk more intelligently with her in his semi drunken state, make her less tempting. The cloak didn't change a damned thing. He knew what the simple garment hid. Too easily he could recall the smooth creamy skin, the soft inviting curves. The searing heat surged anew through his loins.

Anthony couldn't remember the last time he'd wanted anything as badly as he wanted her.

"We'll stay here until morning. Then I'll take you to your…friend."

When she stared at him mutely, he turned back to the window. He'd just resumed plotting his revenge on Nicholas when she spoke.

"Who?" Her voice was small, frightened. "Who sent you for me?"

Unwanted, the image of the horrible bruise at her ribs entered his mind. Her kisses had confirmed the madam's claim of her innocence. The boy's portrayal of her as the victim of a scheming pederast cousin brought into vivid light the fact that she'd weathered much in a short period of time. Including being sold to a brothel.

Anthony handed her the mug of ale he held in his hand.

"Drink this."

Mia accepted the mug and took a tiny sip.

"More," he bade her. "It will calm your mind."

She took another small sip, her eyes never leaving him.

"Lord Claythorne will be happy to see you," Anthony said.

"Adam," she whispered, some of the fear fading from her expression. Anthony felt a rare stab jealousy. "Are you a friend of his?"

"Not exactly." And that was all he needed to tell her.

"He hired you?" she pressed on.

While it was the truth, being in the employ of the dainty young man in question pricked at his pride. Anthony knew he should ignore the question, turn back to the window and spend the night in silence.

Some inner demon wouldn't allow it.

"As a matter of fact, he did," he responded. "And he's paying me very well for your safe return."

Mia nodded, took another drink of the ale. He was impressed with the way she handled the bitter brew. Her gaze focused on some point around his feet as he watched her.

"I suppose it was much too dangerous for him to come alone," she thought out loud. At Anthony's nod, she went on. "Still, I would've thought..."

"Thought what?"

"That he would come for me himself," she explained, her eyes gleaming with unshed tears when they met his. "Even if he had to bring someone with him, I would have thought he would be there."

Anthony shrugged nonchalantly. "Well there is a lot more to consider in his position," he threw out. "There is danger, yes, but there is also his reputation to consider. His family is among the oldest and most respected in England. If he'd come for you and that fact was ever discovered, the scandal would be most damaging. To his family, to his fiancée."

"Fiancée?"

Grateful to Nicholas for sharing that little tidbit, he nodded. "Certainly. She comes from an equally notable family."

Anthony wanted to brush away the tear that spilled over her cheek but wouldn't allow himself to do so. He regretted adding to her pain, but it was best she knew. The more she knew, the better her decisions would be regarding her future.

"Do you love him?" he couldn't stop himself from asking.

"Yes, he's a dear friend. I—"

"Only a friend?" Anthony wanted to know.

Her cheeks colored in the dim light of the room. "Yes, but I had hoped..."

"You had hoped he might be a way out of your circumstances," he voiced his understanding. Marrying the wealthy young viscount would have answered all her problems.

"Yes." Her green eyes dropped to the mug she held before meeting his gaze again. She took another sip. "Isn't that terrible?"

"Not at all." Anthony, if anyone, understood what one would consider when their options were limited.

"So what happens now?"

The healthy drink she took from the mug then had him reaching for it once she was finished. Too much and she'd be ill come morning.

"I'll let you discuss that with Lord Claythorne," he said simply, turning back to the window. "I'll take you to him in the morning." Long moments stretched out. When she spoke again, he didn't miss the bitterness that had crept into her tone.

"You may take me to see Lord Claythorne in the morning, and while I'm grateful for his…efforts to help me, I do not see that I have anything to discuss with him about my future. He can play no part in it."

"He can offer you protection." Anthony knew he fanned her anger. "Make you his mistress."

"His mistress?"

Outrage pulled her to her feet and when Anthony turned to face her he no longer saw the timid woman he'd known so far. Anger deepened the mossy pools of her eyes as she glared at him. Her hands grasped and wrung the costume chain that still connected her slim wrists.

"You lie," she accused. "Adam knows me. He knows I would never agree to such an indecent proposal."

Anthony took a step toward her and was pleased when her ire remained.

"Why not? He's offering an indecent amount of money for your return. Do you not think he will want something for his investment? You know now he never intended to make you his bride."

Mia surprised him by taking a step towards him. Her little nostrils flared.

"Why should I believe *you*?"

"What reason do I have to lie to you?" Anthony pointed out. "My part in this play is over. I've freed you from your desperate situation as agreed. I've no further investment in this."

But he *did* have an interest, so his words weren't exactly truthful. His hard, aching loins could attest to that. The taste of her lips and skin were still in his mouth.

Her eyes searched his face as she considered his words.

"Do you know how difficult it is to be dependent on others for everything? For your very survival? When my father died, I was at the mercy of my cousin. When I became a to threat to him, he sold me into slavery. And now another man is buying me back. I am not a possession to be bought and sold! I am a person! And I want a say in my life!"

Anthony knew pride at her words, even as his body throbbed.

"Then have a say."

"How?" she demanded. "I've two choices. If what you say is true, I can agree to be Adam's mistress or I can live on the streets."

"You have one more option to consider." His eyes locked with hers. And just like that, his mind was made up. He had to have her no matter what he had to do or how long he had to wait. "You can come with *me*."

Her short laugh had an angry bite to it. "And be *your* mistress?"

"No." Anthony began to walk a slow circle around her, leaning close to speak. "You would not be bound to me in any way."

Some of the fire went out of her demeanor. "But you would expect—"

"I would expect nothing," he lied. Of course, he expected to share her bed. But he wanted her to want him, crave him, as he craved her. "Your will would be your own."

"You believe me to be witless?" Her voice sharpened. "You would expect something."

Anthony smiled, his bluff called. "Would it be so terrible then? You enjoyed my touch. I felt it. Why not be with a man who can pleasure you? Who can protect you and give you the freedom you crave?"

"Freedom?"

She smells wonderful, he thought as he lifted a silken lock of her hair and came to a halt before her. He had every intention of making what he offered happen, he realized. She was so beautiful, so perfect. Her inexperienced reaction to his touch promised endless fire and passion waiting to be unleashed. He couldn't imagine tiring of her for a couple of decades.

"I leave France tomorrow as soon as my business is done. I plan to travel far away, to Jamaica. I've been there before, it's beautiful. I can live comfortably there for a long time on Lord Claythorne's reward money. So could you."

Her breath came faster as he pulled one side of the cloak back over one shoulder and planted an open mouthed kiss on her white skin.

"If he truly means for me to be his mistress, he will give you nothing for taking me with you."

Anthony nodded, his lips searing the side of her throat. "We'd have to plan it carefully."

"Plan—"

His mouth closed over hers in a devastatingly gentle kiss meant to coax, meant to entice. She yielded to him after only a moment's hesitation, her full breasts pressing against him as her body began to relax.

Anthony wanted to shout in triumph as her taste, the feel of her, made him spin out of control. She would be his…

CHAPTER 6

"Wait." Mia struggled to break free of his drugging kisses. Planting her hands on the hard plane of his chest, she pushed away from him with all of her might. And it took effort. His amber eyes were dark with desire, determination.

Her mind was spinning. If she were to believe this man, Adam, her one hope in the last few dismal months of her life, was lost to her for any decent arrangement. Perhaps he helped her out of friendship, she reasoned, and that's why he'd hired the dangerous man before her to be her rescuer. But she couldn't imagine Adam asking her to be his mistress. And if he did…

Mia had always thought she could have fulfilled her wifely duties as Adam's wife, though her feelings for him extended only to friendship. But then she had little idea of what that meant exactly. After her experience with the man who still held her in the circle of his arms, watching her intently, she wondered now if she really could have. She couldn't imagine Adam's hands on her body, his mouth teasing her flesh.

But this man, well, he made her feel things that surely weren't decent. The forbidden sensations he provoked were intoxicating and though she was ashamed to admit it, she wanted more. Wanted to let him…

He'd offered to take her with him. That could easily be a lie, she knew. Wouldn't he say anything to get what he wanted? Once he had it, he could easily leave. And where would that leave her?

But if she refused him, would she be any worse off? Her traitorous body wanted him to finish what he'd started, to feel his touch again. If he disappeared the next day, she'd still have no home, no family. No one to care for her.

But she had her freedom. What happened in her life was now her choice. She didn't have to live under the cruel control of her cousin now and she was free of the brothel and its loathsome mistress. And Adam? She'd asked for his help, but he couldn't force her to be his mistress. He had no claim to her at all.

She could choose to let the beautiful stranger before her have his way with her body as easily as she could choose to reject him. For the first time, she felt empowered, free.

"Who are you?" she wanted to know before another thing was said or done.

"Anthony is my name." His voice was soft, as was the graze of his fingertips across her cheek. "And if you knew anything more you would run away in terror. As far and as fast as you could."

Mia nodded her agreement. "I know."

He pulled her against his body, hard.

"No, you don't know." The features of his face hardened. "I've been living in exile here. I'm a—"

"It doesn't matter," Mia said, cutting him off, her decision made. Whatever he was, he would have hurt her by now if that were his intention. Instead he offered pleasure, and she didn't want to live with the regret of having refused him.

Leaning into him, she pressed a kiss to his shoulder, feeling the warmth of him through the linen shirt. Her lips had barely touched his throat when his arms encircled her like steel bands and she felt herself tumbling backwards onto the small, lumpy bed.

Anthony's lips claimed hers in a fiery kiss as his hands worked frantically at the clasp of her cloak. The fabric ripped as he yanked it sharply from her body, revealing her as she had been in the brothel. His breath was harsh as he pulled back to look at her, devouring her with his eyes. His large, rough hands slid under the bodice of her costume, his fingers closed over her breasts, and he lowered himself to her again.

"Mia," he whispered as the tip of his tongue flickered against her lips. He nibbled at her lower lip, his teeth closing gently on the soft curve. Anthony possessed her mouth with slow, intoxicating kisses, pausing to brush kisses on her eyebrows, her temple, her cheeks.

Mia shivered as his lips scorched a trail down her throat to her shoulder. She wanted to wrap her arms about him, pull him closer to her. She struggled awkwardly beneath him with the costume chain.

"I want to touch you," she whispered.

There was a trick to unfastening the manacles and he managed it easily.

Once her arms were freed she slowly wrapped them about him. Never before had she been so aware of a man, the hard muscles beneath the white linen, the power he held in check as his lips and hands caressed her. Mia clung to him as he tore the bodice from her with a savage yank and feasted on the creamy mounds of her breasts. He pulled the points into his mouth, gently biting, suckling, making her moan in pleasure.

It was then that she felt his hand trailing up her thigh to the sensitive cove he'd touched earlier. The bottom of her costume went the way of the top, a scrap of gold flying off the bed. Anthony again took her lips as his fingertips brushed the dark satiny curls at the top of her thighs, lightly at first, then delving deeper into her velvety wetness. Mia gasped into his mouth as his fingers teased and explored her, centering on a spot so sensitive that she nearly threw him off. Relentlessly, his finger teased the center of her pleasure, building again the excruciating pleasure that she'd experienced in the brothel. Only now, she feared she'd expire from it. She needed something…couldn't bear it if he stopped.

His moan was a low growl in his chest as he watched her with amber eyes. Mia jumped when he kissed her ear, so sensitive she was. His warm tongue and breath teased the delicate shell as his fingers continued their gentle assault.

"Would you like me to kiss you there, Mia?"

His laughter was rich and deep at what must have been a shocked expression on her face. But it didn't deter him as he slid down her body, his lips tasting and tantalizing her ribs and flat belly as he went. Mia tried in vain to push him away as he settled himself between her legs. But Anthony wrapped his muscular arms about her thighs, holding her in place and open to him. His warm breath pelted her before he pressed a kiss into the dark thatch of curls.

When his tongue began to slowly stroke her sensitive flesh, Mia knew she would expire from the pleasure. Her hands clutched the coarse tawny locks of his hair, writhing beneath him as his tongue traced the inner petals of her sex. He took his time tasting her, teasing her, finally lapping delicately at the nub where all sensation intensified, making her feel as if she would shatter into pieces.

Mia's cries were barely audible over the din of the bawdy tavern. Something was coming, she knew, as she squirmed in his grip, unable to bear more of his sensual torture. Her body tensed, her nipples tightening almost painfully as the sensation climbed to an impossible summit, then exploded. Strong waves of exquisite feeling washing over her.

His masculine weight moved over her body, and she welcomed it, clinging to him as the intense pleasure relaxed its grip on her. Something hard and hot and velvety smooth brushed her inner thigh as his knees insinuated themselves between hers, spreading them wide. Mia shuddered in anticipation as she felt pressure at her center, felt him pushing his way into her tight, virginal opening. At first the stretching was slightly uncomfortable and he soothed her with soft kisses to her shoulders, her face. Then came sharp pain as he buried himself inside her as far as he could go, sealing his mouth over hers to take her cry of pain.

Mia felt him grow still above her, allowing her to stretch inside to accommodate his incredible length, his thickness. She had no idea if a man was supposed to feel as he did inside her; she only knew that she couldn't possibly bear it if he were the tiniest bit larger.

The pain faded quickly and she relaxed. Anthony obviously sensed the moment she did, and began a gentle sliding in and out of her. Her slick passage closed around him tightly, stroking him as his movements became a driving rhythm that had her writhing again, wrapping herself around him. His kisses were slow, skillful explorations of her mouth as he moved inside her. Mia's fingers plucked at the buttons of his shirt, darting underneath to slide on his slick, warm skin. She felt vulnerable but decadent being naked while he was clothed, riding high on the sensations that were building once more.

Mia clung to him, rubbed herself wantonly against him, as the sensation grew and he hauled her up to tongue her nipple when it tightened to a sharp point. Mia hung onto him as her climax overtook her; she could do nothing else, her nails digging into his flesh. He deepened his strokes at just the right moment, pushed more firmly to prolong her release and she cried out over and over as he held her in place and kept driving on.

Anthony's movements quickened, his arms tightening almost painfully about her. He threw back his head when he found his own release, moaning loudly as he pushed into her one last time and held.

Mia struggled for breath as he rolled off to lay by her side, his own harsh breath fanning her hair. She couldn't remember the last time she'd felt so relaxed and she'd never felt so beautiful, so womanly.

"What is that smile about?" she thought she heard him ask.

But Mia didn't answer. She was fast asleep.

CHAPTER 7

Mia awoke to the sound of the room's door opening and she scrambled to sit up in the bed, to pull the crude quilt up to cover her breasts. A beam of moonlight shone through the room's window to cast light on her, but she couldn't see as her eyes adjusted to the darkness.

"Oh, don't do that." Anthony closed the door behind him. His voice was soothing. He carried a candle in one hand and a cracked blue bowl in the other. Placing both on the table by the window, he said, "No need to be shy now."

Why indeed, she thought, watching him dip a cloth into the bowl and wring water from it. Unceremoniously, he approached the bed and pulled the quilt back to reveal her body.

"What are you doing?" Mia grabbed the quilt to cover herself again.

He blocked her with a powerful forearm. "Let me."

Awkwardly, she allowed him to pull her legs apart and cleanse her where their bodies had joined. The cloth was warm as he caressed her sensitive flesh and bottom with it. She had relaxed by the time he wiped her thighs.

Anthony leaned forward to capture her lips in a light kiss. "How do you feel?"

"It doesn't hurt." She couldn't believe they were discussing what had happened between them. "Just a little soreness when I move a certain way."

"What a blush!" He laughed. "You've nothing to be ashamed of, Mia. What we did was rather tame compared to what you would have experienced at Madam d'Entremont's."

Mia had a hard time believing that. "What else is there?" she wanted to know.

His grin was devilish. "Oh, Mia. There is so much I want to show you, do with you."

She watched him rise from the bed and walk back to the window. He picked up something he'd pulled from his shirt when they'd first entered the room, something wrapped in a dark cloth. He returned to the bed with it, his clothed thigh brushing hers as the bed accepted his weight.

"What is that?" she asked.

Holding it in his open palm he allowed her to pull the cloth away to reveal one of the trinkets from the table of her room at the brothel. The long, smooth object was made of shining glass and oddly shaped—round with a cap on one end that reminded her of a mushroom. Mia carefully lifted it in her hand, studying it.

"I don't understand." She glanced up at him curiously. "What is it for?"

"Allow me to show you."

Anthony pulled her into his arms, dazzling her mouth with a passionate kiss. She clutched the trinket tightly in her hand as his mouth raced down to her nipple, tightening it with swirling touches of his tongue. He pressed her onto her back as his tongue dipped into her navel. He traced wet circles around it before plunging in and out in a mimic of the sex act. His fingers skimmed up her leg to find the moisture at the apex of her thighs. He teased her to bring forth more moisture, more heat. His kisses trailed down her belly, joining his busy fingers, while his tongue devastated the center of her womanhood. He slid first one, then two fingers into her tight body.

Release approached swiftly and she clasped the glass object tighter in her hand. She'd almost reached the summit when he stopped kissing her, touching her.

"Not yet," he whispered as he freed himself from the black breeches he wore and pushed into her, finding her ready to accept him.

Mia gasped as his hot flesh filled her and quickly rebuilt the craving. He braced himself on his elbows above her, watching her face as his body moved in and out of hers slowly, deliberately. Mia's head tossed on the pillow as release approached again.

And again he denied her.

Locking her thighs around him, she tried to pull him back into her but he wouldn't allow it. Instead he took the glass object from her, his gaze intense as he watched her.

"Trust me," he bade her, and rolled the object in his large hands.

Too late she realized what he intended to do. Slowly he nudged the mushroom end of the glass against her opening until she felt it sliding in. Panicked, Mia tried to swat his hands away.

He silenced her with a kiss. "Trust me," he said against her lips. "I will not hurt you."

Mia was uncertain, but she tried to relax as she laid back. Her thighs trembled as the glass slid slowly into her body, filling almost as much as he had. It was hard, unyielding in her body. And not too unpleasant.

"That's right," he whispered, smiling. "Relax. And I'll give you incredible pleasure."

Anthony lowered his mouth to her, his tongue tracing her opening in unbearably light circles all around the smooth glass. Her thighs clasped about his head, the sensation nearly unbearable. He wouldn't allow it. He pressed her slender legs open with his hands and held them wide. He devastated her with his tongue, gently moving the glass in and out of her at the same time until she wanted to jump out of her skin.

He brought Mia to first one climax then another this way, seeming to be in no particular hurry. She believed him to be done with her when he pulled himself up into a sitting position, but he left the glass in place and urged her onto her stomach.

"Please," she begged, "I want to feel *you* now."

His laughter was a low rumble. "As you wish."

She spread her thighs in anticipation as she felt him move her from behind. She waited for him to pull out the glass, wondering if the act could be done with her lying on her stomach. Her answer came quickly when she felt the hot smooth head of him pressing against her, sliding up to her bum and back on the wetness her body had produced. She felt the glass move within her, several smooth strokes. But he did not pull it from her as she expected.

He had something else in mind.

"No!" Mia squeaked as she felt the head of him pressing against her bum, probing into an area she wasn't sure was meant to entertain a man. But he'd anticipated her fright. His weight held her in place as he gently slid into that other opening, causing her to burn and stretch uncomfortably as he went.

"It hurts!" she cried.

"Not for long," he whispered into her ear, his tongue delving into its center playfully. "Relax, Mia. I promise you will like this."

Long moments passed as her body accommodated him in one opening and the glass in the other. One of Anthony's hands slid beneath them to find her flesh, to gently tease the center of her pleasure. Mia began to writhe under his touch, her movements making her aware of the hard glass and his hard body. Slowly he began to move within her, his fingers never ceasing, and Mia clutched the quilt beneath her as intense sensation ravaged her body. More than anything she wanted *him* in her center, not the unyielding, unmoving glass. But as the moments quickly passed, she was crying out, release near. He'd allowed her to pull her legs together, making the glass more of an exquisite pleasure, as he moved in and out her bum. His fingers drove her to madness, as her body soared, powerless to stop it.

Anthony moved in her a few times more before crying out his own release. He slid the glass from her body gently before pulling her against him as he joined her on the bed.

He pressed a kiss into her hair. "Any other questions?"

"No more." She could barely speak, barely breathe.

"Go to sleep then," he whispered. He wrapped her in his strong arms and, overwhelmed by his lovemaking, she did just that.

CHAPTER 8

"I thought she would be with *you*!" Adam Wood's outraged voice rang through the room Nicholas had rented for his stay. "And you leave her all night in the company of a pirate! A murderer!"

Mia's jaw dropped as she looked to Anthony for an explanation.

And if you knew anything more you would run away in terror.

His words from the night before played in her mind as her gaze met his. Anthony's handsome face was a mask of implacable calm, his steady gaze showing no surprise at Adam's accusation.

"Anthony is no murderer," Nicholas Wolfe said, jumping in.

"Of course he is!" Adam's high voice reminded her of a whining child's. "He murdered a woman in cold blood in London!"

Her heart leapt into her throat. How could that be? Her dark lover had murdered someone? An innocent woman?

"Mia, are you all right?" Adam asked with concern as he took her hand and pulled her away from where Anthony stood.

"I'm fine," she said as his blue eyed gaze raked over her.

Anthony had managed to find her a decent muslin morning dress to wear with her torn cloak. He'd brought her fruit for her breakfast, and had slowly made love to her as she'd awakened. He'd murmured endearments to her all the while, telling her he'd protect her always, take care of her.

Was he a killer?

Satisfied that she was unharmed, Adam pulled a great bag from a corner of the room and shoved it rudely at Anthony.

"Take it and leave," he said with a sneer.

Anthony's mouth was a grim line and she could tell he fought himself to keep his silence. His eyes flashed a message to her as he headed for the door with Nicholas.

All you have to do is leave, Mia. Once he's given me the money and I've left with it, leave. I'll be waiting for you.

But did she dare? Was he truly a pirate and a murderer?

Her heart pushed her to run after him, flee Adam's company. Mia's heart sank as she watched Anthony quit the room. Wasn't he the man who'd had the courage to save her from the cruel fate her cousin had planned for her? In a single night he'd taught her about passion, made her realize she had choices after all.

But had he told her the truth about the young man before her who she'd considered a friend?

"I'm so glad you are safe, Mia." Adam took her cold hands in his and smiled. "I was terrified when I learned what Edward tried."

Mia nodded, her eyes searching his. "Thank you, Adam. I don't know that I'll ever be able to repay you for this kindness. But I'm getting ready to start my life over. And if there is ever any way that I can be of help to you, all you need do is find me."

She easily read the confusion in his boyish face. "Find you? Mia, where do you plan to go? Edward still holds your father's lands and wealth. You've nothing. What will you do?"

"I'll find a way," she assured him, watching his ever pleasant features darken.

"Mia," he began, his thin hands clasping her arms. "Be realistic. Unless you plan to work as a servant, you'll be living out in the streets."

"What's wrong with being a servant?" she asked. "It's a noble living."

"You were meant for finer things," he said through his teeth, his growing agitation clear.

Mia smiled at him through her disappointment. "Is that a proposal, Adam?"

She could have laughed at the expression of panic on his face if she hadn't felt so unhappy with his betrayal. And she'd believed him so she had herself to blame as well. The moment stretched out painfully until he finally answered her question.

"I cannot marry you, Mia."

"That's right." She pulled herself free of his grasp. "You already have a fiancée."

His jaw locked. She'd never seen him like that. Gone was her smiling, gentle friend and in his place was a skinny, hard-faced stranger. Mia's heart began to beat out her growing alarm.

"Mia, that doesn't mean we can't be together." Adam again caught her arms in his hands, willing her to meet his gaze.

"That doesn't mean I can't be your mistress, you mean?" she spat, again shrugging out of his grasp. "No thank you."

She turned on her heel to flee, blinking back tears. At least Anthony had told her the truth. She'd just reached the door when Adam grabbed the back of her dress. The fabric ripped in his thin hand as he stopped her from leaving.

"You can't just disappear, Mia." Adam's face twisted into a cruel mask. "Not after what I paid that blackguard to fetch you."

"I beg to differ," Anthony's voice broke in.

Mia's heart swelled with hope as Anthony's fist connected with the smaller man's jaw and sent him sailing across the floor. Adam struggled to pull himself up after a moment. Then his eyes rolled back in his head and he fell limp.

"Anthony!" Mia flew into his open arms, feeling at home. "You were a pirate?"

His expression was grim. "Yes."

"And a murderer?"

Anthony's expression was serious. "I've killed men, Mia. That I won't deny. But the woman whose murder I was convicted of didn't die by my hand."

Mia wanted to believe him, her heart told her to believe. Hadn't he told her the truth about Adam? The hard lines of his face were unyielding, but his amber eyes were gentle as they moved over her face.

"How did she die?" She had to ask.

He swallowed hard before he answered her.

"I was not in time to save her." His voice was low. "She was the widow of a wealthy merchant in London. She and I saw each other for a time. I had enemies, clever enemies. They killed her to get to me and set the stage for my conviction.

"I've never admitted that to a soul, Mia. Not even to Nicholas, my closest friend. I've never given a good damn what people thought. The reason I tell you is because I do care what you think. I want you to be with me."

So much emotion flashed in his eyes. Mia lifted her hand to gently touch his face and Anthony turned his cheek into her palm. The simple gesture telling her he sought her acceptance, absolution.

"I want to be with you, Anthony."

His smile transformed his grim countenance and had her heart racing. He lowered his mouth to hers, promising with his kiss to protect her, to please her. His arms held her possessively and she pressed into him, savoring his heat and strength. In that moment Mia knew that she would follow Anthony anywhere…

And then, hand in hand, they made their way out into the sunshine to begin a new life together.

ELECTRICAL STORM

ELECTRICAL STORM

There were cold droplets of rain in the ocean breeze, dotting Alison Tholl's face and bare arms as she walked along the beach. She wrapped her arms about herself as she walked along the shiny, wet sand. But it didn't help. She couldn't banish the cold emptiness she felt inside.

It had been a year since she last saw Paul Walker's face, since they parted ways on the very beach where she wandered aimlessly.

Alison had flown down to her family's condo at Cocoa Beach on a whim, wanting to return to the scene of the fight just to prove to herself that she was over Paul and didn't need him. Well, perhaps she'd done it up a bit. She wore the same black dress she'd worn that night the year before, ate dinner alone at the same restaurant where Paul had taken her. Hell, she'd even ordered the same meal, had two Tom Collins' just like before.

And now she strolled along the beach alone, remembering that she and Paul had walked together and held hands for a while the night they broke up.

Alison would've given anything if he were there holding her hand at that moment.

Her eyes scanned the horizon, watching the sun setting under angry dark clouds. Storm clouds. Well, that was different from last year. Brilliant flashes of lightning danced along the water in the distance and she watched feeling more miserable by the minute.

She was lying to herself if she thought she was over him. Losing Paul had left a hole in her heart that time couldn't heal. And worse, it was her fault that their relationship ended. Why hadn't she listened to him when he said he needed more from her than what she'd given? Sure, getting tenure at the university where she taught was important. And Paul understood she had to work harder as a woman to gain respect in academia. He'd endured a lot, waited patiently. And what had she done? Not only had she taken him for granted, she'd thrown his marriage proposal back in his face.

His eyes had been so gentle that night when he'd asked for her hand. The tremor in his voice let her know that he was nervous, excited. But she'd been too blinded by ambition to notice. No, she'd panicked with a thousand things that really didn't matter tumbling through her head. Worrying about how soon he'd want children, worrying that he'd insist she took his name. She'd even wondered if the other faculty members would deem him, a mere investment banker, as a worthy spouse.

A low rumble of thunder in the distance kept Alison from walking further. She brushed a lock of dark hair from her eyes as she turned to see how far she'd wandered. *Quite a way*, she mused. She couldn't even see the condo in the distance.

Turning back the way she came, she yelped as something in the sand cut her bare foot. Alison sank onto her heels to find a line of blood along the outside of her heel, just below the rose tattoo she'd had drawn on her ankle only a month ago. The fading sunlight winked off a shard of old, green glass in the sand. Alison angrily flung it out into the water as the ocean gathered strengthening waves.

Well, good going genius. She wore no shoes and dry sand would sting like fire against the wound. If she walked along the water's edge until she reached the condo, though, she imagined the salty seawater would feel little better.

Alison's mood darkened with each step she took and tears stung the backs of her eyes. All she'd accomplished was reminding herself of what she'd had and what she'd lost. She sure as hell didn't feel any better! Her foot stung, her heart ached, and more drops of cold rain began to fall as she made her way back.

Paul, I'm so sorry. I'd give anything to have you back now...

A sharp clap of thunder made her jump and had her looking over her shoulder in alarm. A wide streak of lightning lit up the darkening sky only a few yards behind her immediately followed by another thunder boom. With her heart still racing in her chest, Alison picked up her pace.

But she didn't move fast enough. White-hot light burned into Alison's body the next instant. Everything flashed white before her eyes as she fell to the wet sand. Stunned, she laid helpless for who-knew-how-long as the cold wash of wave swept back and forth under her body. The pain had faded after only a few seconds, but the paralysis was terrifying. Would someone find her? Would the sea wash her away?

"Alison, baby, are you all right?"

Paul!

And there he was turning her over in the sand to lie on her back, worry clouding his deep green eyes. In a second he'd pulled her into his arms, rocked her gently.

"Alison, my God." She didn't miss the fear in his voice, his breath came fast. "When I saw you hit the beach…I thought….I didn't know what to think."

"What are you doing here?" she whispered before she realized that she could. She tried to pull back to look up at him, found she could move. But none of it made sense. Was this real? Or had she died and this was her version of heaven?

Paul frowned, his strong fingers brushed the sand from her face. "Ali, we're on Cocoa Beach. We've been walking…well, fighting…out here for a little while now. Damn it! We've got to get you to the hospital."

"What? Paul, I don't think I need to go to the hospital," she said gently as she struggled to her feet, feeling surprisingly well for a woman who'd just been struck by lightning. He helped her to stand, his large warm hands on her body a sharp contrast with the chilling wind and rain. Reality or not, his touch felt so good. She could feel the warmth of his body as he joined her, standing close; could smell the musky scent he wore.

Alison didn't realize until she stood staring at him just how much she'd missed him, missed his face. Paul had the most beautiful green eyes she'd ever seen. Dark green eyes the color of moss rimmed with golden flecks. He was tall and beautifully muscled with shoulders as wide as church doors. His black hair was neatly cut, longer in the front to sweep boyishly across his forehead. The same shade of black heavily fringed those incredible eyes with thick, glossy lashes. His lips were full and sensual above a strong, unrelenting chin.

Everything about him from the hard planes of his handsome face to the confident stance of his perfectly proportioned body in the sober black suit that he wore filled her with hope, with longing. She caught the burgundy satin panel of his tie on the breeze, savoring the cool slide of it between her fingers. That seemed real. She felt his gaze on hers as her hand pressed lightly to the warm, hard surface of his chest. His heart beat strong and fast against her palm.

"This is real," she whispered, struggling to believe that Paul was there, *really* there with her.

"Jesus," Paul's voice was low as his hands clasped lightly over her upper arms. "Alison, let's go to the hospital. Please?"

"No, Paul—"

"Ali, come on," his grip tightened on her arms.

"Paul…" Her hands rose to his face, her eyes searching his. "You said we've been fighting. What have we been fighting about? Tell me."

Say it, she willed him with her heart thundering in her chest.

But Paul dropped his gaze, remained silent. The warmth of his hands left her as he shoved them into his coat pockets.

Frantically, Alison yanked up the wet hem of her dress, bent low to examine her foot and ankle. Fear and amazement rooted her to the spot. The cut was gone.

And so was her tattoo.

Somehow—she didn't know how—time had ripped open and sent her back to that moment when she'd lost everything. It couldn't be a dream, she had to believe her heart on that one. Paul was there, though his defensive stance told her that something had already transpired between them, hurtful words and rejection. Only concern for her safety kept him there.

It was good enough she decided.

Thunder rumbled angrily in the background as she moved closer to him, slid her arms around his waist. The solid warmth of his body was a homecoming, arousing. She stared up into his face until his gaze met hers and she read the pain there. Pain she'd inflicted on him.

Well, if she could be struck by lightning and travel through time, just maybe she could take that pain away. She'd do anything…

"Paul, I love you."

His eyes closed tightly against her words and he tried to pull away from her, but she held fast.

"Alison, I can't take this," he said. When he opened his eyes again, she saw anger, frustration. "You say you love me, but you prove to me in a hundred little ways that you don't. Tonight I asked you to marry me and—"

She stopped him by pressing her fingers to his lips. It wasn't lost on her that she'd probably been struck by lightning in this reality walking away from him. Their separation had already happened.

"Paul," she said slowly, shivering in the rain that fell hard now. "Whatever I said to you tonight, whatever I made you feel, forgive me. I *do* love you. I can't live without you. Let me prove it," she whispered.

Paul's lips were cold, unyielding when she stretched up on her toes to press her mouth to his. But Alison didn't back off. The opportunity she'd been given was too precious, and she poured her heart and soul into that kiss as the wind whipped around them. Slowly Paul began to respond, his lips acquiescing to the insistent caress of hers, his heart pounding faster. All at once his arms closed around her in a crushing embrace as he deepened the kiss, and Alison knew a moment's hope.

Oblivious to the storm raging around them, they dropped to their knees on the sand, her fingers plucking at his tie, his hands ripping at the bodice of her dress. With a harsh yank, he exposed the soft mound of her pale breast and his mouth dove for it, softly nipping at the hard tip with his teeth before soothing it with quick lashes of his tongue. Alison strained to push herself into his mouth, moaning out loud, joyous as his dark head moved to the other breast, his lips feasting on her. Her hands clutched in his hair as he pleasured her, and she felt like an ancient goddess there with him in the storm.

The deep ache in her hot wet center quickly grew unbearable, and she shoved him backwards with all her might until he sprawled in the sand. His surprise quickly faded from his features and his expression became decidedly predatory as she scrambled toward him, wildly working at his fine leather belt. In seconds she'd pulled down his slacks, the silk boxers, before tugging at her panties. But Paul caught her about the waist with his strong hands, lowering her over him. The skirt of her dress created a warm tent for their lower bodies. Alison savored the feeling of being lashed by the rain above while rubbing her wet heat on the hot silken length of him.

His hands darted under her skirt, ripping away her black panties and diving into the patch of curls to find her clit, teasing it mercilessly. Alison's cries sailed on the wind as the rough pads of his fingers drove her crazy, had her hips working wildly on him. When his fingers delved further, he found her wet, ready passage and groaned. Pulling her head down to capture her mouth for a searing kiss, he entered her body in a single smooth thrust, penetrating her as far as her body would allow.

Lightning lit up the sky as she rode his hard cock, as he bucked beneath her. Wildly their bodies strained towards each other as he took her mouth, suckled her nipples. The waves of Alison's pleasure raged stronger than the sea before her, building with each thrust. Her hands clutched his shirt, her body clenching around him as he stroked himself within her. With a cry heavenward, her climax ripped through her and Paul thrust all the harder, intensifying her pleasure. She gasped as she came down, as he thrust one last time into her body and groaned his own release, his hot passion shooting wildly inside her.

The intensity of Paul's gaze as she struggled to catch her breath kept her heart racing.

"You've never loved me like that," she barely heard him over the rumble of thunder.

Alison grinned at him, feeling triumphant, feeling more alive than she had in a year. "I'm not finished. Let's go back to the condo."

Paul grinned back, and they hauled themselves up from the sand. He worked at pulling up his pants as he chased after her in the rain. She didn't care that her breasts were bared by her ruined dress any more than she cared if anyone had witnessed their lovemaking. Paul was with her, he was hers again. If she had her way, they would never be parted again.

They laughed like children as they ran into the shelter of the condo, closing the door to the storm. The harsh sound of their breathing echoed through the foyer as they stood smiling at one another. Paul found his voice to speak before she could.

"I've got sand up my ass," he said with a laugh. "Perhaps we should think about taking a shower."

"*We* could do that," Alison emphasized.

The steam from the shower felt heavenly against her chilled skin as she peeled off the wet sandy dress and stepped into the shower with Paul. The warm streams of water pelted them both, took away the cold. The golden flecks of his eyes glittered as they moved slowly over her body, making her warmer still.

"My God, you're beautiful," he said as his hands closed over her breasts. His fingers slid down to tease her tight, tingling nipples. "You've never been this way before. So sexy, so abandoned..."

She answered that with a kiss, exploring his mouth with her tongue as his hands explored her body, fingers slipping into her secret cove to tease the sensitive flesh there. His lips burned their way across her cheek to tease the shell of her ear, making her giggle when his tongue dipped into her ear.

"Do you want me again?" he asked.

Alison nodded and those lips devastated her as they continued down her body to tongue her nipples, then dipped into her navel. His tongue deliciously darted in and out of that sensitive little hole in a mimic of the sex act, had her craving his cock inside her again.

Alison shivered in delight as the warm water massaged her back and Paul knelt before her, pressing his mouth to the dark curls at the top of her thighs. When his tongue slid between her folds, she gasped, sinking her fingers into the wet locks of his hair, holding his teasing mouth to her pussy. His tongue licked and laved her clit as first one finger slithered up into her opening then another. Those large rough fingers moved in and out of her in a provocative rhythm while his tongue worried the center of her pleasure. She came hard, her thighs trembling. But Paul was relentless, patiently continuing his ministrations until she came again, her cries echoing through the large bathroom.

Just when she thought she'd collapse in the shower, Paul stood, his hands steadying her. Pressing her back against the shower doors, he pulled one of her thighs way up to sit on his hip before his large, ready cock slid into her body, immediately establishing a steady driving rhythm that had the glass shower doors banging in protest, had her weeping body coming again on his hard shaft. But he kept moving, fucking her as he never had until he threw his head back, driving up into her and holding as his own climax claimed him.

Neither of them were able to speak for a time after that. In the comfortable silence of the bathroom they set about lovingly washing and drying one another. Alison sighed contentedly they headed for the bedroom they always used in the condo and slid under the cool bedsheets naked. Paul snapped the television on with the remote on the nightstand, but his attention wasn't on it. No sooner had Alison settled herself in the bed than he was moving closer to her, his hand skimming up her thigh.

"Are you finished *now*?" His eyes twinkled with mischief.

"As a matter of fact, I'm not," she countered, winking at him.

And with a grand flourish, she pulled the covers away from his body to reveal in him in all his aroused glory. Paul contentedly stretched out on his back, folding his hands behind his head.

Alison settled herself between his thighs and took him in her hands, her fingers wrapping around him. She could probably count on one hand the number of times she'd gone down on him; she didn't really know why she'd not done it more. As she took him in her mouth, teasing him with her tongue as he slid in and out, she realized that she enjoyed pleasuring him—it made her feel powerful. Alison let him slide out of her mouth and began to playfully circle the pulsing head with her tongue.

"Ali," he gasped as she worked on him, his shaft growing harder all the time.

She focused on his pleasure, on driving him crazy, and his hips lifted to meet her, his breath coming fast. He was struggling to reach something in the drawer of the bedside table, but she didn't cease in her work...even when he pulled out her powder blue vibrator.

Alison yelped in surprise when Paul managed to grab one of her legs and began to pull her up the bed. She allowed him to pull her lower body towards him as she continued to tease him with her mouth. Heat warmed her face and she giggled in delight as she realized what he intended to do.

Paul positioned her thighs on either side of his face, his hot breath fanning her curls, making her shiver in anticipation. Before he could touch her with his mouth, she slid her own mouth down on him, taking him as far as she could. He moaned loudly.

He recovered quickly and his soft wet tongue was a decadent treat on her slightly sore flesh. He traced her folds with the tip of his tongue, laved her clit as she continued to work him in her mouth. The position felt so wicked, so good, him teasing her leisurely while she maintained a steady, maddening rhythm on him. The hum of the vibrator made her pause, but before she had time to wonder, she felt the tip of her toy entering her, the delicious vibration nearly bringing her to orgasm as he pushed it all the way inside her body.

While holding it there, he resumed tonguing her clit. She screamed as she came harder than she had in her entire life. Waves of exquisite pleasure washed over her as he moved the vibrator in and out of her several times, growling in satisfaction at the strength of her orgasm.

With an undignified thump, he dumped her on the mattress as he slid from under her body. Paul hauled up her hips from behind and entered her, filling her completely again and again as she pushed back against him to deepen the penetration. Alison arched her back, wiggled her hips as he slid in and out. Another orgasm was coming and she worked for it, waited for it. But just when she was about to come, he pulled out.

She groaned in frustration when she felt him push the vibrator into her body, but gasped when she felt him pressing against her other opening, slowly penetrating where he'd never tried before.

A year ago she would have balked at the idea, would have leapt from the bed. Now she was hot, wanted to come, and shivered in anticipation as he carefully slid into her bum on her own wetness. Her body clenched on the vibrator as he waited for her to adjust to him. It drove her crazy! She wanted him to move, needed him to move. Finally, he took the hint when she backed up against him and slowly began to move in and out of her. For long moments he tortured her pleasurably this way, moving in and out of her bum then ceasing his movement to slide the vibrator to and fro.

"Ali," his breath came hard, "I've always wanted to try this. I…never thought you'd…you'd let me."

But Alison couldn't answer. Her climax was coming on fast with the double penetration. She panted as he moved within her, moved the vibrator, driving her on.

It felt good to scream out her release, felt good to have him groaning behind her only seconds later, his fingers digging into the soft flesh of her hips. Paul pulled out her vibrator, snapping it off as he collapsed behind her on the bed, wrapping his body around hers. She welcomed his weight on her, the feel of his warm, damp skin against hers.

"I love you, Alison," he whispered into her ear.

Her heart shifted in her chest at the words she barely heard. How many times in the last year had she longed to hear those words? How many times had she dreamed of him holding her?

"I love you, Paul." Alison struggled to pull herself up on the rumpled comforter, wanting to see his face. She looked down at him lovingly, her fingers brushing his cheek beneath his closed eyes. "Will you marry me?"

Paul's eyes opened instantly.

"What did you say?"

"Will you marry me?" she repeated with conviction.

Her eyes caught the movement of his throat as he swallowed hard. But she thought she read doubt in his eyes as he pulled himself up from the bed.

"Paul, I've put you low on my list of priorities for too long when you should have been the only thing that really mattered." She spoke her mind and heart. Willing him to believe her, though she'd given him no reason to, she asked "Can you forgive me?"

His lips pressed into a thin line, and he climbed off the bed. She knew a moment's fear as she watched him stalk out of the room. What if he didn't accept her apology? What if he—

But in an instant he was back, a small black velvet box held tightly in his hand. The mattress dipped under his weight as he sat next to her, opening the box to reveal a brilliant diamond ring. The generous stone winked at her from its bed of velvet and she traced its perfect surface with her finger. Tears stung her eyes as she watched him pull the ring from the box with trembling fingers and slide it onto her hand. His eyes gleamed suspiciously as his gaze met hers.

"Yes, I'll marry you," was all he said.

Capturing his face in her hands, Alison kissed him for all she was worth, loving him more than anything in the world. Happiness filled her heart. Paul was back in her life, back in her bed. They would be married, they would have a family. And the bleak year she'd just endured?

Well, she didn't know what would happen next. She only knew that when she settled into his arms to sleep, there was no other place in the world or history that she would rather be.

*   *   *

The sun shone brilliantly through the window as Alison awoke the next morning. The television was still on, a news anchor reporting the happy news that a missing child had been found, alive and safe. And that was a relief. She'd remembered being heartbroken upon hearing about the case before she'd left for dinner alone the evening before…

Alison shot up in bed as the events of the night before filled her mind. Her evening alone, walking along the beach. *The storm!* Had she dreamed that she'd been struck by lightning then? Had she only dreamed of her night with Paul?

Her heart sank in disappointment as she realized that she must have dreamed the whole thing. She was back in the present day and it was highly unlikely that she'd traveled back in time to that night with Paul.

Damn, damn, damn!

She threw the covers back to check the foot she'd cut, to look at her tattoo. She noticed that neither were there about the same time Paul emerged from the bathroom, whistling.

"Did you finally wake up?" he asked, chuckling. "I thought we'd have to cancel our appointment with the wedding planner today."

Wedding planner?

"Paul?" she watched him in disbelief as he approached the bed, a towel wrapped about his slim hips. His dark hair was wet from his shower and there were still drops of water on the smooth planes of his muscular chest.

Concern flooded his beautiful eyes.

"Ali, are you feeling sick again?" He held out a large hand to her. "Do you want me to help you to the bathroom?"

Alison took his hand, solid and real, only to prove that he was actually there. She tugged on his hand until he joined her on the bed, sitting on its edge. Alison crawled into his lap, snuggling close to him. He was real. His arms felt so good around her. She could smell the spicy scent of his soap.

"I'm fine," she said, pulling back to search his eyes. "I'm just so happy to see you."

Paul's laugh was rich and deep, sounding so good to her ears.

"Ali, this pregnancy has you acting very strangely," he said. "And we've got a long time to go yet."

Pregnancy? She was having Paul's baby? Her hands flew to her tummy, finding it slightly larger than normal and tender. The pride in his eyes moved her to tears as she realized she carried a tiny life within her, part her, part him. It was scary, humbling, and miraculous all at the same time.

Kissing her forehead, Paul rose from the bed and walked to the closet to search for clothes. Alison admired the impressive display of muscle as he considered shirts, pants.

"Come on, sweetheart," he threw her a glance over his shoulder. "We meet with the wedding planner in less than an hour."

Oh, my God, it really happened! She actually *had* gone back through time to that night with Paul and had been given the chance to do it better this time, to gain back the love of her life. Memories of her altered reality flooded her mind in an instant. Taking Paul to meet her parents and telling them that they were to be married. Taking him to a luncheon at the university and introducing him with pride to her peers. There were memories of signing a contract when she received tenure, of a pregnancy test that was positive. They'd just bought a house together, she realized. She'd probably gotten pregnant making love with him on their new dining room table.

Why had she ever worried about starting a family? To her surprise and delight, she realized she felt elated at the news that she carried his child. People balanced careers and children all the time these days. And if it proved too much for her, her career would be put on hold.

Alison vowed never to screw up her priorities ever again. She'd love Paul and their children with everything she had for the rest of her life.

She didn't know who or what had sent her back through time, but she sent a prayer of thanks heavenward, more grateful than she could ever express for her new reality. The life that stretched out ahead of her promised to be filled with happiness, love... and lots of sex. She grinned at that, noticing the delicate soreness in her body as she stretched. Her latest memories of making love to Paul were delightful, though he was more careful with her because of her condition than he customarily was.

Paul paused in pulling on his sweater to watch a commercial. Images of tattoos on beautiful women flashed on the screen. Tattoos on midriffs, shoulders...ankles. He shook his head.

"What?" she asked, watching the man she loved as turned he back to the closet and selected some jeans.

"Tattoos," he mumbled. "Why do people feel the need to mark up their bodies like that?"

Alison shrugged as she considered the rose tattoo that she'd never gotten in her new reality. Strangely she could remember that entire year without Paul perfectly though now none of it happened.

And she'd never let herself forget.

Her future lay joyously ahead. They were to be married right here at Cocoa Beach, at the condo. At least a hundred people were coming and she couldn't wait. It seemed so perfect for them to promise themselves to each other there.

"I'm sure glad you never got a tattoo," he broke into her thoughts as he pulled on a pair of jeans.

Paul shook his head again when she began to laugh.

SISTER MOON

CHAPTER 1

Walker Ince glared at the man waiting in the shadows outside his office door. What the hell was someone doing outside his office at this time of the night? It was nearly midnight for God's sake. Not exactly business hours.

But then Walker was hardly working now. It had been weeks since he'd returned any messages from prospective clients. He kept up the rent and the utilities for his office space and that was pretty much it. The private investigation business he'd spent years building was slowly slipping away and he didn't give a damn. His small daughter was dying and only the chance that he had a message from the girl's mother brought him to the office tonight. The rest of the world could go to hell.

And that included the man who moved out into the dim light of the hallway as he approached.

"Mr. Ince, I've been waiting for you."

Walker didn't recognize him. But even in the poor lighting the man struck him as…odd. He was tall and painfully thin with dark hair parted down the middle and a dark colored suit tailored to fit him perfectly. Nothing too out of the ordinary there. But there was something about the way he stood waiting with one hand resting on a walking stick and the other holding a briefcase at his side. He was so still. Too still. And pale, Walker noticed as he came to a stop before him.

"How did you get in here?" Walker wanted to know. Normally, the last people to exit the office building locked the outer doors.

The man grinned at him, his eyes and teeth glittering. His voice was low and smooth as he said, "I walked in."

"Then walk back out." Walker didn't have time for this man and his smart answers. He bypassed the stranger and headed on to his office door, reaching into his jacket pocket for his keys. They jingled as he fished them out, the only sound in the silence.

"How is your daughter, Mr. Ince?" the man spoke again. "I've heard she is ill."

Anger at the reference to his daughter bubbled up quickly as he unlocked the door and roughly pushed it open. Walker spun to face his uninvited guest, glared at him.

"Who the hell are you?" Walker demanded. "And what do you want?"

The bastard was still smiling.

"Just a little of your time, Mr. Ince. Nothing more."

"Time I don't have. Leave." Walker scowled at the man, done with the conversation.

Still, the man didn't move. Hell, he didn't even blink.

"Time *is* a precious commodity, Mr. Ince," the man continued as if he hadn't been asked to leave. *Twice.* "I have way too much of it and your daughter has too little. But perhaps, with your help, we can even the distribution."

"I don't know how you know about my family," Walker used his most menacing tone, "but if you dare—"

"Mr. Ince," the man interrupted him. "Please. I was simply searching for someone with your particular skill set to help me with a very important matter. When I learned of you, I also learned of your daughter's plight. I am sorry for her illness, but it only convinced me that you *were* the man I was looking for. I think we can be of great help to each other."

Walker had always been a cynic. He didn't like the slick look of the man any more than he liked being approached by a stranger about so personal an issue. His gaze dropped to the briefcase the man held at his side.

"I don't need money," Walker said simply.

The man's dark brows rose ever so slightly.

"I'm not offering you money. I'm offering you a cure for her."

Walker tried to fight back the small glimmer of hope in his heart at those words.

"Yeah, right," he tried to sound nonchalant.

"Just a few moments of your time." The man motioned towards

Walker's office. "Please."

He didn't want to spend one more minute with the strange man, much less invite him into his office. He wasn't accepting jobs right now. Why the hell should he talk to him?

But what if...

The doctors had given his poor Melody only weeks to live. The cancer had been discovered the week of her third birthday when he'd taken her to the emergency room for stomach cramps that wouldn't go away. The terrible disease had ravaged her little body in a matter of months. They'd tried everything, approved and experimental. No one and nothing had given them any hope.

Looking at the determined set of the man's inky black eyes, Walker wanted to know what he thought he could do for his daughter that the best doctors could not. He wanted to throw him out by the seat of his tailored slacks, never see him again.

What if?

The desperation of a father had him nodding and stepping back to allow the man to enter his office. Walker followed him in and closed the door. He knew he was only asking to be disappointed again. But the possibility, no matter how remote, that someone could help Melody... Well, he'd regret it to the day he died if he didn't at least hear what the man had to say.

The man headed straight for his desk, making himself at home in one of the large leather chairs in front of it. Walker made his way around the desk to take a seat in his own chair, snapping on the lamp between them on the desk as he sat down. The soft light illuminated the sharp features of the man's unnaturally white face, highlighted the intensity in his black eyes. The man quickly opened the briefcase on his lap and produced a red folder. Placing it on the desk in front of Walker, he opened it to reveal a photograph of a young woman.

It was a black and white surveillance photo taken of her while she waited for something or someone. There were a lot of people in the background. It appeared that she was standing on a busy street corner, probably waiting for a bus or a cab. That was as far as Walker's analytical mind got.

The sheer beauty of the woman captivated him. Her face was all delicate curves and angles with a dainty nose and full sensuous lips. A wealth of long curls framed her face and long sleek neck perfectly, just reaching the soft swell of her breasts. The simple blouse and skirt she wore showed off her figure—her small waist and long, long legs.

With the tip of his finger he traced the top of her head, wondering about the color of her hair.

"Who is she?" Walker asked, still staring at the photograph.

"Her real name is Emma Hurst." The man's dark eyes darted from the photograph to Walker's face, his expression one of implacable calm. "She has used many aliases, but she always sticks with the same initials. The last alias she used was Emily Hauser."

"You've been following her for a while, huh?" Walker threw out.

"Indeed I have."

"Who are *you*?" Walker wanted to know.

"My name is Julian Beart." Sitting back in the chair, the man sighed. "I've been following this lady for a few years now. She has something of mine. Something precious to me."

"How did it come to be in her possession? Did she steal it from you?"

Julian Beart's eyes narrowed. "It was stolen from me, but not by her."

"Does she know she has it?"

"Yes."

"Does she know that you want it? That it belongs to you?"

"Certainly."

Walker already didn't like where this was heading, beautiful woman or not. Wanting to cut to the part where his daughter was supposed to benefit, he exhaled impatiently.

"Have you ever simply asked her for it?"

The man's laughter rang out rich and loud in the quiet office. "We've talked. Let's just say that it didn't go very well. But that's funny. That's the first time anyone has ever asked me that."

"Look, I'm in the investigation business." Walker met the man's gaze squarely. "If you can prove that whatever she has is yours, you would be better served by calling the police."

"Does it really have to come to that? As I mentioned *she* is not the one who stole it from me. I don't want to see Emma incarcerated." Julian leaned forward and pinned Walker with an intent stare. "Emma doesn't have to be hurt. I just need you to retrieve the talisman from her."

"Wait a minute." Walker held up a hand when the man went to look into his briefcase again. "This doesn't make sense. If she knows she has this item and she knows it is yours, why would she not give it to you?"

"Two reasons. She's been misinformed, and she doesn't understand exactly what it is."

And with that he produced a color photo of a golden pendant around a lady's neck. The pendant was in the shape of circle with a smooth blood red stone at its center. It hung from a thin chain.

"The talisman has great powers, Mr. Ince."

Walker's heart started hammering when he read the headline from the yellowing newspaper the man placed before him next. A photograph of a smiling boy was situated below the words *Local Boy Miraculously Recovers From Brain Tumor.* The newspaper was dated April 13, 1991.

"Take a look at this." Julian's voice stopped him from reading more about the boy from Redding, Connecticut and his overjoyed family.

Julian Beart produced a small magnifying glass and held it over the picture of the boy in the newspaper article. The glass revealed something hanging around the boy's neck. It appeared to be the same pendant in the other photograph the man had showed him.

"That boy's tumor disappeared overnight," Julian explained. "Much to the doctors' amazement..."

"And that necklace cured him of that?" *Was it possible?*

"Yes, the talisman rid him of the tumor, Mr. Ince. But you have to know how to use it as I do for the miracle to happen."

Miracle? If only...

"This doesn't prove anything," Walker said more for himself than for the person he was speaking to. "Sure it looks like the same necklace. But I don't believe in magic or talismans, Mr. Beart."

"At the moment, perhaps not." Julian Beart smiled at him. There was emptiness in the man's eyes and it forced a cold chill down Walker's spine. "But you will."

Walker fought the crazy mix of hope and apprehension that had his heart racing and his mind scrambling. He had never been the superstitious sort. And he sure as hell didn't believe in magic necklaces or lucky charms.

"The choice is yours." The man's soft voice broke into his thoughts. "You can retrieve the talisman, return it to me and save your daughter's life. Or you can choose not to help me and let her die."

Melody was going to die. It was the one thought he couldn't bear, the fear that he lived with every day. There was nothing he wouldn't do to give his little girl a chance to live.

But was he willing to put his faith in the odd man who rose from the chair on the other side of the desk?

"What's in this for you?" Walker asked.

"I don't have as much at stake as you, obviously." Julian Beart gently placed the briefcase on the desktop, laying it on its side with the handle facing Walker. "Everything you need to find Emma is either before you or in this briefcase."

Walker's heart was hammering in his chest now, the sound of blood rushing in his ears as he tried to get his mind around the entire situation.

"I'm an investigator, not a thief." Walker shook his head. "What am I supposed to do when I find her? Rip it from her neck?"

"I have little doubt that you'll think of something. And I'd recommend doing so before the next full moon which is three nights from now." The man's eyes gleamed like obsidian. "The full moon brings out the worst in our Emma."

"What the hell is that supposed to mean?" Walker watched him turn his back and head for the door.

Julian Beart laughed again. The sound had Walker grinding his teeth in annoyance.

"Yes, you are the perfect man for the job," he said before slowly opening the door and walking out.

Just like that he was gone. Walker exhaled and slumped back in his chair, his gaze falling on the briefcase in front of him. Curiosity about its contents had him sitting up again and pulling it towards him. He lifted the lid to find the briefcase was filled with neat stacks of money.

I knew it.

The question was what to do now.

Melody smiled at him from a photograph in a shiny golden frame beneath the small lamp. His little girl before the illness, with her eyes bright and her hair gleaming…

The boy from the newspaper article smiled up at him, too. A boy who'd supposedly been cured of a brain tumor years ago by the necklace he'd been asked to retrieve.

Was it possible that necklace could cure his daughter?

Despite the reservations he had about Julian Beart and his promise of a miracle cure, Walker pulled out the photograph of Emma Hurst and studied it for a long time.

CHAPTER 2

Emma Hurst smiled as she watched the group of women at the table nearest the bar break out into fits of laughter at something one of them had said. They were probably around her age, early thirties. And they were having a good time as women always did when they had the chance to break away from their lives to visit with each other. She shook her head when one started complaining about her husband's fishing trips. Didn't he know there were a lot of things he needed to do around the house? Another one chimed in that hers stayed at the house and that wasn't necessarily a good thing because he drank beer and watched sports all of the time.

As she wiped down the bar, she shook her head. These women at least had men they loved and all but one of them had mentioned having children. It was a lot more than she had. *Do they have any idea how lucky they are?*

But Emma didn't want to hear what they were saying any more than she wanted to hear the two men at the end of the bar talking about the "chicks they banged last night." Or the couple in the back corner of the room bickering over what to do about the woman's unexpected pregnancy.

She couldn't help it. It was *that* time of the month. And boy did that have a different meaning for her than it did for most women on the planet.

Emma had been born a werewolf and had long ago accepted it. What choice did she have? Every month as the full moon approached, the changes came. Her senses gathered strength, *she* gathered strength, until the full moon when the *big* change occurred. But the next morning it was over, she was back to her old self and the whole process started again.

And, all things considered, it wasn't enough to keep her from living a somewhat normal life and having all the things that other women had. If she found the right man, who loved her and could accept what she was, she could have a life like the women at that table. Children were a trickier subject. But she could even live with never having children of her own, if she had love. There was always adoption.

But finding love was a little hard when you lived on the run. Even if she managed to find someone, it would only be a matter of time before *he* sent the next assassin after her. Julian Beart would never rest until he had the talisman back, would never leave her alone. Emma resented being its guardian, but she was the last of her line. There was no one else.

She'd almost finished college when Michael died and the burden of the talisman passed to her. Since then she'd stuck to the larger cities, using false names to pick up mostly bartender jobs. Once in a while she did other things, like work in video stores or small shops. Emma would go crazy if she tried to hide away in the country somewhere, waiting for Julian to send someone to kill her. Better to be out in the open, surrounded by people. Bartending was her favorite way to be part of the world, and behind the bar she always had the best view of the rooms she worked.

Throwing the hand towel over her shoulder, she tried to block out the voices of the women who'd moved on to complaining about their jobs as she went to the kitchen for clean glasses. A man was sitting at the bar waiting for a drink when she returned.

Oh, my. What a man. Sandy-haired, handsome, with a bold nose, a hard sullen mouth, and pale blue eyes. He was an undeniably masculine creature, possessing a swarthy complexion and dominating physical presence that made her feel almost tiny. His broad shoulders filled out the dark leather jacket he wore over a deep red sweater, and his large hands were lightly clasped on the counter as he waited. The skin of his hands looked rough, was littered with small scars. He wore no wedding ring, but she knew from experience that didn't necessarily mean anything.

"Hi there," Emma greeted him.

Those pale blue eyes met hers and excitement coursed through her body. His gaze roamed over her face and her hair. Emma released the breath she hadn't realized she'd been holding. He smiled at her, deepening the cleft in his strong chin. She had the insane urge to touch that indent, to run her fingers through the silky locks of his sandy hair.

"Hi there." His voice was deep and smooth. "I'd like a vodka and tonic please."

The intensity of his gaze had her fumbling with the bottles of vodka and tonic water. For an instant she could have sworn there was a hint of recognition in his eyes.

Please don't let Julian have sent him.

And then she noticed the smell on him. The smell of sickness and pending death. She'd know it anywhere because of Michael's illness as a child. *Cancer.* But the man before her showed no sign of any illness or weakness. He was as virile and full of life as anyone she'd ever met.

"You have the most beautiful red hair," she barely heard him over the din of the crowded room.

Emma nearly dropped the lime slice in her hand at his words. Somehow she managed to secure it on the edge of the glass despite the fact she felt giddy as a schoolgirl. She slid the drink across the counter toward him and tried to tuck the strip of white hair at her temple behind her left ear. It was habit.

He watched her over the rim of the glass as he took a drink, and there was laughter in his eyes.

"You turned quite a shade of pink," he pointed out.

Emma laughed nervously. "Well, you jarred me out of my routine. *I'm* supposed to say something charming and you laugh. That's how it goes. Now I don't know what to do."

His smile widened. "You could tell me your name to start with."

Careful now. "Emma." He didn't need to know the last name she'd been using lately.

"Emma," he repeated, holding out his hand. "I'm Walker Ince."

Pleasurable currents went up her arm the moment she took his hand. Emma thought he meant to shake it, but he surprised her by turning her wrist and pressing a kiss to the back of her hand. His lips were warm, lingering for a moment, and Emma melted. Desire ran through her body like rivers of hot lava flowing toward the softening apex at the top of her thighs.

Slowly she pulled her hand back and tried to regain her composure. It was pretty damned hard with Walker Ince ignoring his drink and staring at her so intently.

"Is there not enough booze in your drink or are you just happy to see me?" Emma teased to break what was, for her, an uncomfortable silence.

He laughed, a low rumble in his chest. "Actually, I was thinking it was a shame that the most beautiful woman in the bar is the one keeping it."

Okay, he's really cutting to the chase. That had her pulling the towel down from her shoulder and wiping the perfectly clean, perfectly dry bar with it. It was just what bartenders did. Gave her something to do besides standing there staring at him like a love-struck teenager anyway.

"Well, it's not a bad place to be," she returned. "I'm not one to pick up guys in bars."

Emma had used the comment before and it usually made her point with all except the really drunk.

But Walker's smile widened. "I'm not one to pick up women in bars."

"So what are you doing here?" Emma asked before she could stop herself. *Idiot! Judging from that smell, he's probably here because he knows someone who is dying and needs a drink to deal with it.* "Sorry. Not my business."

Some emotion she couldn't name crossed his features, but it was gone in an instant. "That's okay. So neither of us pick up people in bars. We already have something in common."

"That only comes in handy if you plan to get to know someone better," Emma pointed out, still absently wiping the bar.

The longing in his eyes as they dropped to her lips pinned her to the spot. "I hope that's the way it goes."

A wave of pure lust tightened her nipples into diamond hard points. The sensitive flesh between her thighs twitched.

"Hello there!" a female voice broke the spell.

Emma begrudgingly moved down the bar to take the order of a young couple sitting a few seats down from him. But she could feel his eyes on her the entire time. She hurried to make drinks for her other customers, not stopping to chitchat as she normally did. No, she had to concentrate because Walker Ince was quite a distraction.

It would have been better if he'd just moved on or left, but he waited as she dealt with her other customers. *This can't go anywhere,* she told herself. But she wanted it to in the worst way. Her body had been on red alert since he'd caught her eye. And, of course, the drink umbrellas, fruit sticks, and straws were under the counter right where he was sitting so she was forced to walk by him often. She could almost feel the force of his desire from the other side of the counter. His eyes darkened to the color of a summer evening sky.

"Emma."

Scrambling to give change to the businessman at the end of the bar, she glanced back over her shoulder at Walker and nodded. She expected to meet his heated glance as she walked toward him, but she found him staring down into his drink instead. For a moment he looked *...sad?* But the instant she stopped on the other side of the counter, he looked up at her and the devilish glint was back in his eyes.

"You haven't finished your drink." Emma tapped her fingernail on the side of his glass. "Or did you just want the pleasure of my company again?"

Oh, *that* earned her a grin to mess with a girl's insides.

"Knock 'again' off the end of that and it will be an accurate statement."

Emma gripped the edge of the bar. She melted under his heated stare and her panties were damp already.

"When do you get out of here?" he asked.

The direct approach. She liked that.

"Midnight," she tried to sound casual.

Walker glanced quickly at his watch. "Thirty minutes."

"Why?" she had to ask.

He started to speak and then stopped. Emma's heart hammered as she wondered what he'd been about to say. Did he want to take her home or go home with her? What would she say if he did? Hell, she'd never had a one-night stand in her life, but the handsome devil before her was a powerful temptation. *I just might. God, I want to.*

But the old familiar fear crept into her mind. *She couldn't take him home with her. What if Julian sent him?*

Yet Walker Ince just wasn't Julian's style. He was the total opposite of the cold, calculating mercenaries he'd sent after her in the past.

That may have been Julian's intention.

"I just want to talk to you." He spoke slowly, looking her in the eye.

Damn!

"For a start."

Emma's knees shook behind the counter, and she was grateful he couldn't see them.

"Where?" Emma asked. "Not many places open in Bar Harbor after midnight."

"Looks like a nice stretch of shore down from Acadia." Walker's eyes searched hers. "I know it's chilly, but I won't keep you long."

This gorgeous sexy man and a moonlit shore? Her heart said yes, her body said *please.*

And her rational mind warned her to think about it. If by some chance Julian *had* sent him, how easy would it be for this powerful man to take the talisman and dump her body in the ocean? Her hand flew to her chest to feel for the pendant under her blouse.

His gaze followed the motion of her hand as she felt the shape of the talisman beneath the fabric. She panicked. *What if? What if?*

"I-I'd like to, but…it's been a long day," she explained. It was a pretty lame excuse.

His eyes closed tightly…in regret? When they reopened, they met hers and he nodded. He pulled his wallet out and slid a ten-dollar bill across the counter to her.

"I understand. Have a good night, Emma. Maybe I'll see you again soon."

Walker's eyes met hers squarely as he rose from the barstool. The desire and longing in his gaze were undiminished.

Her heart squeezed in her chest as she watched him walk away. She couldn't help but notice the back of him looked good, too. *He has a nice ass.* Emma waited, hoping he'd look back at her, but he didn't.

Damn! Damn! Damn!

Chances were she just let the most amazing man she'd ever laid eyes on walk away. And yet in another corner of her heart she felt relief and that bothered her. Why would she feel relieved? Because it would never have the chance to develop into more and really break her heart?

Or because she was afraid Julian *had* sent him?

The scent of sickness that had clung to him still lingered in the space he'd occupied.

Emma shook her head, told herself to forget him as she set about closing down the bar for the night. *Nothing would have become of it.*

But she knew she wouldn't be able to forget Walker Ince.

* * *

Two hours later Walker slipped into Melody's hospital room in Bangor. The nurses had left the light on over the small steel sink as they always did, and he quietly walked up to the hospital bed where his daughter slept.

She looked so tiny in the bed with its metal side rails, hooked up to monitoring machinery on either side. His fingers brushed over her small head. Gone were the shiny dark locks of her hair, only tufts were left growing here and there. Her skin was no longer rosy but ashy in color and there were deep shadows beneath her eyes.

Walker shrugged out of his jacket and pulled up a chair to the edge of the bed and sat down to pull off his shoes. He took her small hand in his and his sleeping child turned towards him to curl on her side.

He prayed the same prayer he'd said every night since Melody had been diagnosed with cancer. He prayed for her to be spared at any cost to himself. Walker would have given anything to take her place, to know that she would live even without him. *His* mother would be there to care for her, to raise her.

Melody's mother had left them for another man when their daughter was only a year old and had gone to live with her lover in France. She'd promised for weeks now she'd come to be with Melody and every day his daughter asked for her. But he knew Stephanie wasn't strong enough to take it. Though he didn't expect to see her at all, he still tried, calling her every day for Melody's sake.

But the image of another woman's face drifted into his mind for the hundredth time tonight. Emma Hurst had his head spinning, made him feel so many things…

Walker had studied her photograph for a while before realizing that the corner of the brick building behind her was a place he'd visited many times in Bar Harbor. Once he'd reached the seaside town, he'd spotted her instantly, walking into the small restaurant and tavern in her little uniform with its simple white blouse and black vest and slacks.

Whether he'd meet a conniving con artist or a scared rabbit, he hadn't known. But he'd been totally unprepared for the beautiful, warm woman he'd discovered tending the bar. He squeezed his daughter's hand, thinking how much of a sharp contrast she was to Melody. Emma was so vibrant and alive, with her fair creamy skin and her shining auburn hair. He'd turned as hard as steel the instant she smiled at him and he hadn't completely squelched the surge of lust she'd inspired in him. *Him.* It was amazing, because Walker had felt dead inside for weeks, watching his daughter fight a losing battle.

His reaction to Emma had caught him off guard. And it was the only excuse he had to offer for coming on as strong as he had to her. He couldn't blame her for blowing him off at the end. But it put him in a bad position for the next step.

And there would be a next step because two things had become crystal clear to him during their exchange. Though he never saw it, he believed she had the necklace Julian Beart wanted, had been *wearing* it beneath her white blouse.

And for whatever reason, it meant something to her. The fire in her eyes had faded with the color in her face when she'd pressed her hand to her chest to verify that it still hung there. He thought he'd read fear in her lovely green eyes as her fingers found it and she backed out of meeting him after work.

Fear of what? Had Julian threatened her in the past?

There was something to Julian Beart's story after all, he could feel it. There had to be something to the damned necklace if Julian wanted it so badly and Emma apparently did as well.

That meant there might be hope for Melody.

The course was set. He had to see it through now.

But the stunning redhead complicated matters greatly. Would he simply take it from her? What if he simply tried to talk to her? Just tell her why he needed it. What if *she* could use it to cure Melody?

He, Walker Ince, was contemplating how best to get a supposedly magic necklace from a beautiful bartender. It was madness.

What the hell do I do now? Walker buried his face in his free hand as he sat by Melody's bedside. No matter what happened now, he instinctively knew Emma Hurst would be hurt by it. Walker didn't like that thought at all.

Melody hummed in her sleep as he laid his head on the mattress next to her. His child came first, no matter what. He *would* get the necklace.

Sleep didn't come easily to Walker. And when it did, Emma Hurst's beautiful face haunted his dreams.

CHAPTER 3

The next day was rainy and it matched Emma's mood—cool, moody, and gray. She had several errands to run and took her time about it. But not because she hoped to run into Walker Ince. It was time to have the oil changed in her car anyway, and she'd been meaning to open a new savings account at the bank. She went to the post office to buy stamps because those she could always use.

The uncomfortable platform heels? Okay, she wore those in the hopes she ran into Walker Ince. And they were killing her feet. It was all she could do to limp across the street from the garage where they still worked on her car.

Emma made her way towards a small restaurant with bright red lobsters painted on the windows. Two waiters stood under the awning outside watching her as they smoked. She couldn't decide if they were staring at her or her Speed Buggy umbrella.

Once in the restaurant and seated at a small table next to the window, she sighed in relief. She was off her aching feet and the bowl of clam chowder she ordered would take care of her growling stomach. Hauling the spaghetti strap of the sundress she wore up on her shoulder, she gazed out the window at the busy street.

The smell. The instant after she noticed that familiar scent of sickness mingled with the scent of man, the scent of *him,* she felt the strap of her dress being pulled back down her shoulder by a large rough finger. A thrill of excitement raced down her spine at the slow unexpected touch.

Walker.

Emma looked up into his pale blue eyes. The intensity in them had her heart pounding. Walker Ince's sandy hair was disheveled from the wind and rain. He looked amazing in a blue buttoned down shirt the same shade as his eyes and faded jeans that fit him so well nothing was left to the imagination.

My, my.

"Emma?"

His tawny brows rose slightly in question and warmth flooded Emma's face at having been caught staring at his…*package? Unit?* Ah, hell, she felt giddy just seeing him again.

Clearing her throat, she sat straight in her chair. She could at least *try* to be a lady, couldn't she?

"Hi, Walker."

A corner of his mouth pulled up into a sexy half-smile. "Want some company?"

"That would be great." She sounded too interested, too perky. *Damn it!* "I just ordered lunch."

Walker slowly sank into the chair across from her and thanked the waitress who'd rushed up to offer him a menu. He ordered an iced tea before turning that heated stare back on Emma. Jolts of excitement raced through her body under his gaze.

The light of day revealed little details about him, the faint lines on his face. There was a thin white scar on the high slope of his cheek.

"What's good to eat here?" he asked.

Well, there's me…

"This is only the second time I've been here," she answered honestly. "I remember the clam chowder was excellent. That's what I ordered."

Walker nodded, dropping the menu to the table. His smile was teasing.

"You should be checking out the competition more often than that."

"Well, I haven't been in town that long," she blurted. *What the hell made her say that?*

"I knew you weren't a native. You don't have that charming local accent," he pointed out.

Emma smiled at that. Having been born and raised in the south, she struggled sometimes with the very different accents of New England and their rapid delivery. But she wasn't about to tell him that. She wouldn't tell anything about herself that she didn't have to. Just to be safe.

If you want to play it safe, then get the hell away from him...

"You're dressed warmly for a summer day." Emma directed the conversation toward him. It was a tactic that usually worked well because most people loved talking about themselves.

But instead of the inane round of babble she normally got, his gaze drifted deliberately down from her face to her breasts and slowly back up.

"You're dressed *beautifully* for a summer day, Emma."

His hands slowly slid against each other on the table before him. Strong hands with long fingers moving smoothly back and forth in a way that fascinated her, had heat pooling low in her belly. How would those fingers feel against her nipples? The sensitive flesh between her thighs warmed and softened just imaging the glide of those fingers against her clit, dipping inside her.

Damn him! He made it impossible to have any normal conversation. No matter what she said, he came back with something personal, something to set her nerves on edge.

The waitress arrived with his iced tea and her bowl of soup. Walker returned the menu to her and ordered a club sandwich without completely taking his attention from Emma.

"You have a way of keeping me completely off balance," Emma said, half teasing, half serious as the waitress walked away. "Do you know that? You show up at my bar and you look at me like you are now and... Why are you looking at me like that? What do you want?"

"I just got here," Walker pointed out, laughing.

Emma laughed with him. Because of nerves? Because she wanted to jump his bones?

Walker's laughter faded. "I can't take my eyes off you. But if I told you what I wanted, you just might kill yourself on those shoes trying to get out of here."

Fear mixed with excitement, pushed her desire to an exquisite level. Her thighs squeezed together, pressing into the damp cotton of her panties, and her heart raced.

"That depends on what you want." She tried to sound flippant but didn't quite make it. "Do you want *me* or do you want something *from* me?"

His lower lip twitched as his eyes searched hers.

"Honestly, both."

It was difficult to breathe. *What did he mean both? What did he want from her?*

He wanted *her.*

And she definitely wanted *him.*

"You make me feel so much that I'd forgotten," he said in a low voice. His hand slid across the table to capture one of hers. Her hand looked tiny in his. The firm stroke of his thumb back and forth across her palm created pleasurable waves that traveled throughout her body. "I want know how it feels to hold you, how you taste. I want to lose myself inside you."

Emma's lower lip trembled. So did the heated flesh between her legs.

Was it worth the risk? What if Julian sent him? What if…?

The full moon was tomorrow. Emma's strength grew as the full moon came on. If by some chance Julian *had* sent him, and her lust was leading her down the primrose path to danger, well, she could handle it. She didn't want to believe Walker Ince had anything to do with Julian or would ever harm her, but… It wouldn't be the first time she'd been in danger since the talisman had come to her.

It *was* the first time she'd ever decided to have sex with a man who was practically a stranger to her. But she'd never so instantly wanted any other man. Ever. It was intoxicating.

It feels good.

Curls of steam rose from the bowl of soup, but her hunger for food was gone. Now she only hungered for him. Her fingers closed around his teasing thumb, capturing it.

"Let's go."

*   *   *

Since the mechanics hadn't changed the oil in Emma's car yet, they took Walker's SUV. Apprehension kept Emma from taking him back to the small house she'd rented. Instead, she directed him down a little known road not far from Acadia National Park. It led to a quiet stretch of shore that teenagers used for the same reason she was about to. *To have sex!*

Walker's warm hand closed over her thigh as he drove, squeezing gently. In a smooth, quick motion he clasped her thin skirt and yanked it up her leg, exposing the sensitive flesh of her thigh. His touch was unbearably light, his fingers skimming higher until they found the damp cotton of her panties. He moaned deep in his throat as his fingers stroked her through the thin material and Emma spread her legs to give him greater access.

Having reached the end of the road, Walker brought the SUV to a halt and quickly shut off the engine. His eyes met Emma's for a split second before he leaned toward her, his mouth capturing hers in a searing kiss. Emma's mouth opened under his, allowing him to explore her mouth with his tongue as his hands sank into her hair, then skimmed down her body. Her passion matched his and she savored his taste. She wrapped her arms around him, her hands sliding all over the muscled wall of his back.

His rough hand grazed her skin as it slid down her neck to the top of her sundress. Since the strap already hung uselessly across her arm, it was easy for him to tug the bodice of her dress down to reveal her breasts. Her nipples were tight, ready points aching for his fingers and his mouth.

But the talisman was also revealed and Emma held her breath, waiting to see what he would do.

Walker groaned and seemed not to notice, dove for her with his mouth. An exquisite shot of pleasure raced through her body straight to her mons as his lips spread over one aching peak, teasing her with quick lashes and flicks of his tongue. Her hands slid into the silky locks of his hair as he moved to the other breast. Relentless in his passion, he sucked her nipple into his mouth and Emma felt the gentle pull in her warm, wet center. She wanted his touch there, wanted him inside her. In a frenzy, she pulled his hand from her bodice and directed it down her body until his fingers slid inside her thin cotton panties.

Walker moaned against her breast as his fingers sifted through her curls to find the tender lips within. Emma arched her back as a single finger slid into her folds, sliding on her wetness up to her clit. His touch was slow, amazing. Her fingers clutched in his hair and her thighs closed around his hand as he teased the sensitive little nub with light strokes, matching the rhythm of his tongue on the equally aroused point of her breast. Emma gasped and writhed in the seat under his ministrations as the tension built in her body and the pleasure threatened to overwhelm her.

Then he stopped.

Emma cried out in protest even as he pulled her from the seat towards the bench seat behind the driver's side. His breath was coming fast and his face was flushed.

"I want to taste you, Emma."

Walker pushed her down on the seat, sliding her panties down her body before her head rested on the vinyl. He sank to his knees in front of the bench as he whisked her underwear off. Emma yelped in surprise as he leaned across her abdomen, spread her open with his hands and claimed her with his mouth.

Helplessly, she clung to him, finding and gripping him through the tight denim. His lips and tongue teased her nether lips on their way to the center of her pleasure and had Emma gasping in ecstasy. The weight of his upper body held her hips in place, and that was no small feat considering Emma was ready to come, and twisting wildly beneath him. Walker was hard as steel, but much hotter under the denim, and she tried more than once for the button of his jeans, the zipper, anything. But it was hard with his amazingly quick and stiff tongue tracing circles around her clit and teasing her ready passage at turns. Her hips shot off the seat when his tongue began to lash the stiff little nub, and the more she thrust herself up at him the more ruthless he became.

She held on as long as she could, but all of her nerves were on fire, and currents of flame were running through her limbs to the quivering flesh between her thighs that Walker teased and tormented. Emma's cries filled the vehicle as the orgasm shook her. She rode out the sweet spasms as Walker fumbled with the fly of his jeans. He climbed onto the seat between her gaping thighs and pushed the jeans down his slim hips.

His cock was long and ready. He entered her in a single smooth thrust and Emma moaned her delight as her flesh gave way for him. Her sheath still trembled from her orgasm, little tremors that he must have felt, too. His eyes squeezed closed as he gripped the seat above her with one hand and the vinyl at her head with the other for leverage.

"Emma," he groaned as she wrapped her legs around his waist and he began a steady driving rhythm within her. His stiffening flesh pressed the walls of her passage and she clenched around him with each thrust. She plucked at the buttons of his shirt, clutching at his heavily muscled arms in her passion. His thrusts were pushing her up the seat. Emma held onto him as he threw his head back, driving into her desperately.

Walker filled her, consumed her. The slick push and pull of his cock within her quickly pushed her back towards the edge of pleasure and her thighs clutched his hips tightly as the next climax came, her fingernails raking his back through the fabric of his shirt.

"Walker," she gasped as she came hard, her center liquefying around him as he drove on above her like a man possessed. His body grew tense, his thrusts harder. Pale blue eyes filled with fire bore down into hers as he allowed himself release and his body jerked from the intensity of it.

His breath was a harsh rasp as he gently pulled her up into his arms, his cock easing out her as he did. His heart beat furiously under her palm as he held her, pressing kisses into her hair.

"So much fire," he whispered against her ear. "I thought you'd burn me alive."

Emma struggled to breathe, too. Their lovemaking had not only left her breathless but had seriously heated his SUV.

"It's hot as hell in here," he said between harsh breaths. "The windows are up."

Walker pulled up his jeans while she hauled up her bodice. They scrambled back up to the front of the vehicle and hastily jumped out of the passenger door, laughing like children.

Emma smoothed out the skirt of her dress and followed Walker to a grassy area shaded by tall maple trees. Since her legs were still shaky, she sank down onto the grass, enjoying the way the prickly cool blades felt against her skin. She felt wonderful, sexy, and satisfied.

Smiling, she glanced up at Walker who joined her in the grass, stretching out with his hands tucked under his head. The sunlight filtered through the leaves of the trees, speckling him with light. He looked different to Emma in that moment. She didn't realize until she gazed down at his serene features how much intensity had been there before.

"What are you thinking?" Emma asked.

His blue eyes shifted from the canopy of leaves above them to her.

"I was thinking…that this is the first truly peaceful moment I've had in a very long time."

Emma smiled down at him. "If I had anything to do with that, I'm glad."

"You have everything to do with it." His sigh was long and deep. "I'm falling for you hard, Emma. I just wish…"

Happiness mixed with a little dread at his words had her heart picking up speed. "You just wish what?"

"I just wish that I had met you before now." Walker's eyes searched hers. "Under different circumstances."

"Because of the something you said you wanted *from* me?" Emma wanted to know, her heart pounding in the silence as he paused.

Walker's expression was stilled and serious. "No, that doesn't have anything to do with it at all. I just wonder what it would have been like to have met you last year, or the year before."

"Why?" she pressed. "You aren't married are you?"

He chuckled. "No, I'm not married. I'm divorced and I have a little girl. All I meant was, that I'd have loved to have met you at a happier time in my life."

"Why have you been unhappy?" she wondered out loud. He'd been married and had a child. Had the marriage ended badly? Was he unable to see his daughter often?

Walker shook his head. "Not right now. I don't want to talk about it right now."

Her fingers toyed idly with a button on his shirt.

"I guess talking about that something you wanted from me is out of the question," she tried to sound teasing though she was dying to know.

"Damn right it is," he said in a playful tone. There was nothing playful about the way his gaze roamed down to her lips, moved slowly down her body. "Kiss me."

A thrill of excitement ran through her body as she leaned over him and pressed her lips to his. Her hair fell all around them as their lips played lightly together and Walker's hands slid up into her hair, holding her in place for his gentle kiss.

All at once he stopped, pulling back to look at her.

"Is this deliberate?" he asked, his fingers twining around the strip of pure white at her left temple.

Emma shook her head. She'd been asked that before. But now in Walker's arms, with all the passion she felt for him and all the unknowns about him, she felt self-conscious and uneasy. Like him with her earlier questions, she didn't want to talk about it. She didn't want to invoke the memory of how that strip of white had come about and how her father had died.

"I don't want to talk about it right now," she gave his own words back to him.

His brows knitted. He started to speak, but Emma pressed her fingers to his lips before resuming their kiss. His mouth opened under hers and she took the opportunity to explore him, to taste him. Emma plucked at the buttons of his shirt, undoing them, and he groaned as she brushed kisses on the indent in his chin and down the warm flesh of his neck. She teased the hollow at the base of his neck with her tongue and she could feel the tension gathering in his body, feel his hands clenched in her hair.

With all of the buttons undone, she pulled his shirt back and pressed soft kisses to the flat muscular planes of his chest, teasing his nipples with her lips and tongue until they were hard and tight. She knew she liked that. But when she continued down over his flat stomach to the top of his jeans, he groaned. His hands slid down her body, the fingers of one hand sliding under her skirt to find the damp curls at the apex of her thighs. The tantalizing glide of his fingers into her sensitive folds made it difficult to concentrate on the fastenings of his jeans, but she managed to unfasten them despite his pleasurable assault. The pad of one of his fingers stroked her clit in a way that made her push herself into his hand even as she pushed down his jeans and took the length of him into her mouth.

Walker's teasing fingers hesitated as her tongue traced circles around his head. His eyes darkened with desire as he watched her hands and mouth work on him. But slowly he resumed his ministrations under her skirt as she loved him with her mouth using long, slow strokes. His hips rose to meet her as she took him into her mouth again and again, taking as much of him as she could each time. Emma's body wept its desire onto his caressing hand, his fingers sliding easily on her wetness. His touch renewed the craving in her body, making her want him inside her again.

Emma lifted her mouth from him and hiked up the skirt of her sundress as she straddled his slim hips. Walker held his cock in place for her to lower herself onto it and she was so wet she slid down easily.

"Ride me," his voice was husky.

Gripping her hips in his large hands, he urged her into a steady rhythm up and down on him. Her passage tightened around him. Emma moaned in delight as she planted her hands on his smooth chest and rode him hard. Ripples of excitement coursed through her as he filled her again and again.

"Emma." Walker's breath came fast. One of his hands slid up her back to pull her down to him for a searing kiss. The new position offered exquisite stimulation for her clit since he rubbed against her with each thrust. Her fingers clutched as his shirt as his tongue explored her mouth and he continued to drive upward inside her. Another climax was coming and she wanted it, *needed* it. He seemed to realize she was close because his thrusts quickened, increased in strength.

Her sheath quivered around him and she cried out into his mouth as she came, stunned by the power of her release and the intense pleasure from it. She wrapped her legs around his waist as he rolled them over so that she was on her back. He lowered his body to hers, thrusting wildly until the sensations gathered anew in her body. Emma held him in her arms, holding on as his fingers worked their way between their bodies to find her clit. She tightened around him, inside and out, waiting for the explosion. When it came, they rode it out together, their cries mingling in the quiet open space.

After a long moment while they fought for their breath, Walker started to lift his weight from Emma, but she held him tight. He lifted his head anyway, his blue eyes meeting hers.

"What are you thinking?" he asked in a soft voice.

"That this is the first truly peaceful moment I've had in a long time."

A wide grin split his face. *God, he's handsome.*

"You're a bartender, for crying out loud," he teased. "Can't you think of something original to say?"

"Not when I'm around you," she said honestly.

Walker kissed her chin. A butterfly kiss. Emma couldn't remember the last time she'd felt such happiness.

CHAPTER 4

Walker's heart felt like a weight in his chest as he stepped back into Melody's room. His daughter was weakening, the doctor had explained in hushed tones in the hallway. It was only a matter of time before her major organs shut down, until…

He refused to accept it. The numbness he'd felt for the last several weeks was gone, lifted from him like a heavy cloak. He knew that Emma had a lot to do with that. She moved him, made him feel again. When he was with Emma, it was bliss.

But as he stared down at his sleeping child, his feelings were pure agony, raw and hurting.

He had to talk to Emma about the necklace *today*. Guilt washed over him as he considered the time he'd spent with Emma in the woods the day before. Selfishness had prevented him from asking her about the necklace. He'd chosen to just make love to her, to enjoy being with her, and forget the heartbreak and despair that had held him prisoner for so long when he should have been asking her about the necklace.

What if it really *could* save Melody? What if something had happened to her while he was with Emma?

Walker sank into the chair by Melody's bed as she turned to face him. Her little eyes opened, shining bright blue in a tiny, pale face. His heart shredded in his chest as she smiled at him and held out her tiny frail arms.

"Daddy!"

Moving to sit on the edge of the bed, Walker gently took his daughter into his arms. "Hi, princess."

Melody pulled back to peer up at him. "I missed you yesterday."

Tears stung the back of Walker's eyes. He'd not spent any time with her the day before while she was awake. "I missed you, too. What did you do yesterday?"

"I drew you a picture, Daddy." Pulling away from him, she reached for a colored piece of paper on the table on the other side of her bed.

Walker reached over her head for it to help her and his heart lurched when he gazed at the picture she'd drawn in black crayon. It was a stick person she'd drawn and that wasn't so unusual. But the fact that she'd only used the color black, when she had at least a hundred crayons in all colors, and that her stick figure had a walking stick had his blood running cold.

"Who is this, honey?"

"That's the man who came to see me. He said he was your friend, Daddy."

Julian Beart. Why had he been in his daughter's hospital room?

"What did he say, princess?" Walker's heart was racing. "Do you remember?"

"He told me that you were going to get something that would make me feel better today," Melody's eyes shined at him with hope.

That son-of-a-bitch! Furious that the strange man had dared come to his daughter's hospital room, Walker's fist tightened on the paper.

"Did he say anything else?" Walker fought to keep his emotions from his daughter.

But Melody had always been perceptive. Worry crept into her expression as she nodded. "He wanted me to give you something."

From under her pillow she pulled a small business card and handed it to him. In small neat handwriting it read *I'll be back at midnight tomorrow, Walker. For the talisman...*

"What's it say, Daddy?"

"It says he will be back tonight to talk to me," he said through gritted teeth.

Melody laid a small hand on his arm, tape holding the needles in the tender, bruised flesh for her IV and medicines.

"What do you want me to tell him, Daddy?"

Pulling her against his heart, he fought his emotions and sent a single prayer heavenward. *Don't let anything happen to her until I get back.*

"Don't you worry about that, princess," he whispered into her hair.

"I'll be here when he comes back. I'm going to have to go out again. Just for a little while, okay? I'm going to call Uncle Denny to stay with you? Would you like that?"

Melody pulled back to smile up at him. "Yeah!"

Denny Link had been his best friend since high school. Melody loved him as much he did. Walker knew Denny would do anything to protect her. That he was the local sheriff didn't hurt matters right now.

"I'm going to ask him to come play with you while I'm gone, princess." Walker kissed the top of her little head. "I won't be gone long."

"Okay, Daddy."

Walker reached for the phone on the table at his knee and dialed Denny's office. Once Denny or someone arrived to ensure Melody was safe, he had to find Emma.

* * *

Emma had just reached the door of the tavern where she worked when a blaring car horn drew her attention. It was Walker's SUV and he was motioning her toward him.

Smiling as she remembered their evening of lovemaking the day before, she walked in his direction. But her smile faded as she reached the open passenger window and saw the grim expression on his face. What had happened since she'd seen him last?

"Get in," his voice was low.

"I've got to work." She motioned back toward the tavern with her thumb.

"Emma, please."

Dread squeezed her heart with tight painful fingers as she stood there staring at him. Whatever was wrong had to do with her and that had her wanting to turn around and run for the tavern. That she'd gone and fallen in love with him, she wouldn't deny. She should have known something would go wrong. He was going to break it off with her for some reason, she just knew it.

Or Julian had sent him.

Shit!

"Emma?"

Taking a deep breath, she opened the door and climbed into the passenger seat next to him. She was thrown back against the seat when he romped on the accelerator and sped off down the busy strip. Her heart lurched in her chest as she struggled to put her seat belt on. A man walking across the street started sprinting, a couple of elderly ladies gawked at them in fear as they flew by.

"Walker! What's up?" she asked in a shaking voice.

But he didn't speak as they reached the little road she'd guided him down the day before. He stared ahead in stony silence until they reached the shady grove and he brought the vehicle to an abrupt halt.

Emma watched him climb from the vehicle and march over to the shade of the trees. He was pacing back and forth, raking his hands through his hair by the time she climbed out on her side and headed towards him.

"Walker, what's wrong?"

Icy fingers of dread squeezed around her heart as she watched him. Emma could feel the tension gather in his body from where she stood.

"Emma you asked me if I wanted you or something from you in the restaurant yesterday," his voice was low, had the slightest tremble to it. His blue eyes locked with hers. "Do you remember what I said?"

Adrenaline rushed through her and she was surprised to feel the signals of the change coming on. *The full moon was tonight, but she shouldn't be changing yet.* Emma fought it, her limbs beginning to tremble. She didn't know what he was going to say to her, after all. He might say anything. *It could be a thousand different things.*

"You said both," Emma answered.

Walker nodded. "It started out as one thing. I wanted something from you. Wanting *you* wasn't part of the plan, but when I found you, when I saw you… God, I need you so much. You feel so good to me, Emma."

Emma swallowed hard. "What is the something you want, Walker?"

She didn't want to ask that question, didn't want him to answer it. The sound of blood rushing filled her ears as she fought to keep her composure, fought to suppress the triggers in her body. The blood of the wolf trying to take over…

"I think you know, Emma," he said, his eyes fastening on her chest as if he could see the talisman beneath the white blouse of her uniform. "You're a smart woman."

Julian had sent him! The realization made her feel that the breath had been knocked from her lungs.

"Julian Beart sent you?" she whispered.

The pain on Walker's face was easy to read. He nodded.

"Walker," Emma said slowly, "I don't know what he told you, but I need you to listen to me. I need to explain—"

"What is it?" he cut her off. "What is it exactly and what does it mean to *you*?"

Pressing her fingers to the small pendant above her heart, she met his gaze squarely.

"It is a talisman, Walker," Emma explained. "It's been in my family for hundreds of years."

Walker shook his head. "He says it belongs to him."

"Part of it does." Emma stepped towards him and unbuttoned the top two buttons of her blouse. With trembling fingers, she reached for the talisman and held it up for his inspection. "Do you see the red bead at the center? That is a drop of his blood."

"Yet it's been in your family for hundreds of years?"

The skepticism in his eyes and voice stung. Sure, they'd only known each other for a short time. Had what they'd shared so far mean anything to him? Fear mixed with a sense of betrayal and it was a bitter pill to swallow.

He's normal, Emma reminded herself, *an ordinary man*. It must have sounded like a pretty wild tale to him.

"Yes." Emma struggled to keep her voice calm and steady. "He's a warlock, Walker. He's a male witch, a very powerful one. I don't know how old he is exactly, but an ancestor of mine somehow got a drop of his blood and sealed it into this pendant. He's powerless without it, bound to whomever possesses the talisman. As long as I am its guardian *he* can't harm me. But that hasn't stopped him from sending others, Walker. It never stopped him from arranging the deaths of those in my family for generations."

Walker shook his head again. Emma could read the growing disbelief in his expression.

"Emma, I'm going to tell you right now that I have no intention of trying to hurt you. My client said he didn't want to see you hurt either."

Emma snorted.

"That's the truth," he said evenly. "He just wanted me to get the talisman from you. What he told me about this necklace seemed a little farfetched. But warlocks? That live for hundreds of years?"

Was that pity in his eyes? Emma's anger flared fast. Did he think she was crazy?

"My ancestors didn't know he would live on and on when they bound him," Emma snapped. "But he has. And he can't be released."

His eyes narrowed as walked slowly around her in a half circle.

"Let's say I bought your story." Walker's voice was gruff. "Why did your ancestor bind him, as you put it? What happens if Julian Beart *is* released?"

"Don't you think this is hard for me to believe, too?" Emma couldn't keep the frustration from her voice. "I wasn't there when this all went down. All I know are the stories that were told to me by my mother, Walker. Her father told her. You know as well as I do how things get added or lost in the translation as stories pass from one person to another."

"What stories?" he prompted, coming to a stop before her.

Please believe me, she willed him as took a deep breath.

"My ancestors came from a small village in France. My mother told me that Julian Beart was a disciple of the devil. Supposedly he kidnapped and killed little children and used parts of their bodies in his rituals."

The color drained from Walker's face. *Good.* Just maybe she was getting through to him.

"The people in the village were good people, Christians. They believed the devil lived among them. When the body of the village leader's son was found mutilated, he rallied his neighbors in his grief and they tried to burn Julian alive in his dwelling. But he got out and he cursed each and every one of them, making them into terrible creatures."

His blue eyes searched hers, his expression stilled and serious. "Creatures?"

Emma's heart pounded so loudly that she knew he must have heard it. "Werewolves, Walker."

He opened his mouth to speak, but Emma jumped in before he could.

"Walker, that village leader was my ancestor. I don't know how he managed to get that single drop of Julian's blood. But I do know he hoped Julian would eventually just die. But he didn't, and as the generations passed, the fact that he lingered on and on, unchanged, only convinced those in my family of the need to keep him prisoner at whatever cost."

"Emma, this is crazy." Walker took a step back. "Do you know how crazy this sounds?"

"Yes! I do, but—"

"Are you telling me you *believe* this?" he cut in. So many emotions crossed his features. "Can you prove any of it?"

Her limbs were shaking violently now and Emma could only guess that her upset had triggered the change to come on early. She wrapped her arms about herself, fought it. She had to make Walker understand, because he was in danger from Julian, too…

"I can't *prove* anything, Walker." Her voice was shaking now. "But you have to trust to me. I have reason to believe everything I just told you."

Walker took another step back from her, shaking his head. But his eyes softened as they moved over her face and he reached out to her to cup her cheek in his hand.

"Emma, are you ill?" he asked carefully.

Don't pity me, damn you! Don't pity me!

"Tell me something, Walker," her voice shook badly, she was barely holding on. "What's in this for you? Did he offer you money?"

Slowly he shook his head. "My daughter has cancer, Emma. He told me that necklace could cure her. Just like it cured another boy ten years ago. She's not going to last much longer. She's only four years old."

His voice broke on the last. And Emma's panic began to quicken the transformation.

The nightmare was happening all over again. Her half-brother Michael had been born to their father a human, no trace of the wolf in him. He'd only been seven years old when they'd discovered the brain tumor. Her father had been the guardian of the talisman, but hadn't believed the old tales. He had, however, believed Julian Beart's lies. It had been the perfect setup for Julian. Her father had the talisman and Julian had Michael as his human sacrifice.

Blood was shed to bind him, blood must be shed to make him whole again.

A sacrifice was required to return Julian to his former strength and the blood of the innocent had the most power. The blood of a child. She'd never forget that day when she'd walked into Michael's hospital room. The day her father died…

Walker's daughter!

It was too late to tell him now. Emma felt her body begin to convulse. The change was coming and there was nothing she could do about it.

Walker's hand slid down and he captured the talisman in his fingers at the same moment her stomach clenched and she doubled over. The chain gave away and Emma managed to look up to see Walker staring at her mutely with the talisman in his hand, the chain dangling from his fingers.

No!

"Emma?" his voice was muted in her head. "Are you okay? Emma?"

But she couldn't answer him. The spasms brought her to her knees on the grass. Her bones began changing and thick fur began to push its way through the skin all over her body, the feeling like thousands of sharp needles piercing her. Emma cried out in pain, a preternatural growl, as she fell onto her side. Her body contorted and convulsed, the seams of her blouse and slacks ripping as the blackness came to claim her. Her chance to make Walker understand the danger they were all in was lost now. Walker knew now what she was. And the talisman…

Walker had the talisman!

It was the last thought she had before she passed into unconsciousness.

CHAPTER 5

Holy shit!

Walker ran as fast his legs would carry him to his SUV, the necklace clutched tightly in his hands. He jumped into the driver's seat, locked the door and started the engine, throwing it into gear and gunning the accelerator like the hounds of hell were chasing him.

It wasn't far from the truth. Walker watched the gray wolf in his rear view mirror as he raced up the narrow road, and so far she was keeping up with him. *It was Emma.* He'd actually *watched* the woman he was falling for, the woman he'd made love to, turn into a wolf of all damned things! It had been a terrifying sight and Walker wasn't easy to scare. He could still see her lifting herself from the ground, her teeth bared and her eyes glowing with menace as she stared at him.

He made it to the highway and sped up as he pulled out onto the smooth, straight strip of road. He didn't think she'd be able to keep up with him for long, but a glance in the mirror revealed she was running alongside the rear wheel on his side, her ears flat against her head as she ran. Walker's chest tightened in alarm, in regret, as he kept one eye on the road and one eye on Emma. The speedometer showed he was traveling at ninety-four miles per hour.

The setting sun gleamed off a car coming towards them. Walker's heart jolted in fear as he considered that Emma was right in its path. He broke out in a sweat as he watched the car approach. Just as the car was about to reach them, Walker steered into their lane. The car's horn blared as they gave him a wide berth, running completely off the road.

Walker's SUV fishtailed as he struggled to pull it back into his lane at the high speed. Panicked, he searched the rear view mirror for Emma and spotted her behind him in the road, merely trotting now as if the near collision had frightened her.

But she appeared unharmed.

Walker slowed down, but still drove faster than he should have as he headed for Bangor, still checking his mirrors every few seconds for any sign of her as he drove. But she didn't reappear. Eventually his heart slowed, but he couldn't shake the feeling of foreboding.

The pendant was captured between his hand and the steering wheel, imbedded into his palm. The fact that he had what he'd came for brought him no satisfaction, no peace of mind.

It was insane what he'd hoped for yesterday, that he'd be able to just talk to Emma and work something out. The moment he'd walked up to her table in the restaurant he knew that wasn't possible. He'd craved her, *had* to have her. And he'd read the same desire that rocked him in her eyes. Emma had been like nothing he'd ever experienced, so much fire and passion.

What a difference a day makes, he thought bitterly. Since yesterday Julian Beart had been to his see his daughter in her hospital room, and Emma had stunned him with her wild story that his client was hundreds of years old and that he was an evil warlock who was bound to her family by the necklace. While his rational mind told him she just might be crazy and her story was impossible, in his heart he wanted to believe her. And not just because of the stunt Julian had pulled with Melody.

He loved Emma.

But she'd turned into a wolf before his very eyes. *A wolf!* He'd seen werewolves in movies. But they weren't supposed to be real!

Walker wondered if he was losing *his* mind.

No, he had to *think*. Julian Beart had sent him after a talisman and the woman who claimed it. He told him that he would use it to save Melody, he even hinted that Emma was a werewolf. He told Walker that Emma was misinformed, that she didn't understand what the talisman actually was.

But if Emma's story were true, that he wanted the talisman back to regain his strength, how could he use it to help his daughter? Why would he want to?

Not knowing what to believe, he focused on what he *knew*. He had the necklace and they both wanted it. Emma would come for it because she believed she was its keeper, believed she was protecting mankind from a warlock. Julian Beart would want it, too.

But why, if not for the reasons Emma had given him? Julian had said it was precious to him, but never stated exactly *why* he wanted it. He'd admitted to following Emma for years, admitted that he'd talked to her once and it hadn't gone well.

... supposedly he kidnapped and killed little children and used parts of their bodies in his rituals...

Walker's heart raced as he finally reached the hospital parking lot and climbed out of the SUV. The sky was darkening under a rising full moon as he sprinted across the parking lot and into the hospital lobby. He sped through the hallways, nearly knocking over a nurse walking her elderly patient, to get to Melody's room. When he reached it, he threw open the door, startling the nurse who stood checking one of the machines by his daughter's bed and Denny who sat dozing in a chair by the window.

Marching up to the bed he found Melody resting, blinking like a sleepy owl. Walker smiled at his little girl, brushing a kiss on her forehead.

"Hi, princess," he whispered.

"Hi, Daddy." Melody stretched and yawned. And then she smiled up at him, her small hand cupping his cheek. Her little hand was so cold.

"Have you had fun with Uncle Denny?" he asked gently. "What did you do?"

Denny smiled at her indulgently, but Walker read from the tense lines on his friend's face that the situation was hard for him.

Melody nodded, her little eyes shining out at him from her small wan face.

"We drew pictures, Daddy. See?"

Walker shuffled through the series of drawings of flowers and castles, relieved. He glanced up at his friend. "Any trouble?"

Denny shook his head. "So what's going on?"

There was no way he was going to try and explain this to Denny. Not that he'd believe him anyway. Walker couldn't get his mind around the entire situation himself and he was in the middle of it.

"A client spooked me is all." Walker was going to say as little as possible. "I just wanted to make sure Emma was safe since I had to run that errand."

He could read curiosity in his friend's eyes, but Denny let it go.

"You okay now?"

Walker nodded, shaking his friend's hand as he rose from the chair. "Thanks, man."

"Any time." The sadness his friend felt was in his eyes. He clapped Walker on the shoulder before walking around him to kiss the top of Melody's head. "Bye, Melody."

"Bye." Melody waved to him as he walked out and gently closed the door behind him. She yawned and reclined on her bed.

"Are you sleepy?" Walker asked.

Melody nodded and closed her eyes. In seconds she was asleep. He stood there and watched her as he always did to make sure she was still breathing, still with him. She slept so much now...

"Walker."

Emma. It was impossible.

But Walker turned to find her standing behind him with her beautiful hair disheveled and dressed in hospital scrubs. There was a long cut across her cheek.

"How did you get here?" he asked.

Emma's small smile didn't reach her eyes. "I ran."

Closing the hospital door behind her, she moved towards him. He watched her flinch as if he'd struck her when he moved to block her view of Melody.

"Walker—"

"So you can change from a wolf and back whenever you want to?" he wanted to know, folding his arms across his chest.

"Not usually," her voice was low. "Normally it is just the full moon that brings it on. The next morning I'm myself again. But this—"

"What do you while you are a...wolf?" he cut her off again.

She shook her head, her eyes searching his. "I don't remember. But I've always barricaded myself in my house when it happens. I've never hurt anyone that I know of."

The fear in her eyes was easy to read. "Walker, we don't have much time. It's almost sunset. I'll be changing again soon."

Her voice sounded pleading and he wanted to go to her. Wanted to comfort her, to hold her. But he stood where he was, unsure.

"Do you still have the talisman?"

Walker unfolded his arms and opened his closed hand to reveal it to her. She made no move to take it.

"Please don't give it to him," she begged.

"Emma, I want to know one thing. Can this necklace cure my daughter? Can it save it her?"

Walker's heart pounded fiercely as he waited for her answer. Her green eyes were so gentle as they shifted from him to the bed where Melody slept and they were glossy with gathering tears.

"No, Walker. It can't."

His chest tightened painfully as his hopes were dashed yet again. It wasn't the answer he was hoping for. Reaching into the pocket of the jacket he'd left in the room earlier, he pulled out the folded newspaper article Julian Beart had given him.

"Then what about this?" he wanted to know, holding it out to her. "That boy is wearing that necklace in the picture if you look closely."

Emma's hand shook as she took the paper from him and unfolded it. Her eyes scanned the page for only a moment before lifting to meet his.

"Michael was my half-brother, Walker," she began slowly. "He wasn't like me …he was human. Our father loved him very much and would've done anything for him when they discovered the brain tumor. Just like you are willing to do anything for your little girl. But Michael died from that tumor. This is just one of Julian's illusions."

Emma blew on the page she held and it burst into flames in her hands before disappearing altogether.

Startled, Walker's hand closed around the talisman tightly, his heart racing as he waited for her to continue. He didn't make a move to stop her when she walked around him to stand at the foot of Melody's bed. Instinctively he knew she wouldn't hurt his child. Tears slid from her eyes as she gazed down on his daughter, lost in her memory.

"My father didn't believe in the stories, though he was a werewolf himself. It was so easy for Julian. He told my father the talisman would cure Michael, made him believe it. And he almost succeeded in getting exactly what he wanted that day."

Walker didn't want to know the rest but he had to hear it. The sky beyond the hospital window was growing dark. "What do you mean?"

"My grandfather once told me that blood was shed to bind Julian and blood must be shed to make him whole again. Julian needs more than the talisman to restore his powers. He needs to shed blood, a human sacrifice. When I walked into the hospital room that day, my father had just given Julian the talisman. I watched Julian hug my father." Emma crossed her arms before her as she relived the scene. "And then Julian stabbed him in the neck with a strange looking knife. He died instantly."

Emma swiped at her tears with the back of her hand. "I was terrified, Walker. I just cowered in the doorway as he approached

Michael in the hospital bed. He needed Michael's blood for his ritual. The blood of a child has the most power. But when he saw me, his face changed. He looked grotesque, demonic, like nothing I'd ever seen. I don't know how I did it now, but I just grabbed the talisman from his hand and he ran away. He still had that horrible face...that's what happened to my hair..."

Fear knifed through him at her words. He reached her in an instant, grabbing her arms and forcing her to look at him.

"Are you telling me you think he means to use my daughter as his human sacrifice?"

Tears ran freely down her cheeks, but she looked him in the eye and nodded. "Please, believe me. He's coming."

Walker swallowed hard, his eyes shifting to Melody and back. "If I give the necklace back to you..."

"He'll still come," Emma explained. "I didn't come here for the talisman, Walker. I came here for you. I love you. I don't want him to hurt you or your daughter."

Dragging her against him, Walker held her close to him, his heart beating against hers. It wasn't fair. He'd finally found a woman to love and his world was going to hell around them.

But one thing Walker vowed. He might lose Melody to death, but it wouldn't be at the hands of the lying bastard who was coming that night. Walker didn't give a damn what Julian was or what he could do, he'd see him rot in hell before he'd let him touch a hair on Melody's head. Or Emma's...

"Is there any way to stop him?" Walker asked.

Emma winced as if from great pain, her arms wrapping about herself just as they had earlier. He knew what was about to happen. Tilting her chin up as she began to shake, he asked again, "Can we stop him?"

"Use... his magic against...him," she managed. "That's all I know."

Her fingernails are turning black!

Walker pulled her over to the hospital window and slid it open, urging her to go through. If she turned into the wolf there, she wouldn't be in control of herself. She could be hurt. Or she could hurt someone else, and he knew she didn't want that.

"You have to get out of here, Emma. Go!"

Squeezing through the window, she scrambled across the grassy lawn behind the hospital toward a wooded area close to the interstate.

His heart went out to her. He hoped she would be safe, that Julian wouldn't go after her.

But *he* had to protect Melody. He would do whatever he had to do to keep her safe.

Julian Beart was coming.

*   *   *

"Walker, I've come to finish our business."

The digital numbers of the clock flashed 12:00. Walker watched Julian Beart quietly slip into the hospital room. He was dressed just as he had been three nights before, walking stick in hand. But there was a gleam in his black eyes as he walked toward the hospital bed where Walker sat next to his sleeping daughter. It drove a spike of fear into his heart, but he fought it.

"Let's finish it," Walker tried to sound casual.

"Do you have the talisman?" Julian asked, grinning.

"No," he replied. "I'm sorry. I couldn't get it from Emma."

Julian's smile faded and he took a step closer. "What did you say?"

"I said I didn't get it," Walker clearly and slowly pronounced each syllable of his lie. "I don't think I can help you. Our business is finished."

Even in the dim room Walker could see color creep into that unnaturally white face. Julian Beart's eyes narrowed as they fastened on the pocket of the shirt he wore.

"Why are you lying to me?" he asked calmly. "The talisman is in your pocket."

Walker sighed, made an effort to look bored though every muscle in his body was tensed and ready for action. It had the effect he intended as he watched Julian's hand clench around his walking stick until his knuckles turned white.

"If it were, how would *you* know?"

Julian's laugh was a cold ugly sound in the silence of the room.

"Didn't Emma tell you?" With a great yank, Julian pulled the handle from his walking stick to reveal a long, sharp silver blade. He pointed it right at Walker's heart. "I'm a warlock!"

Julian sprang into action, dodging just in time to avoid being skewered by the deranged man crashing to the floor at the foot of the bed. Pulling his .32 from the waistband of his pants, he shot Julian in the chest just as he pulled himself up from the floor. Julian laughed at him, ripping his shirt open so Walker could see the bloody bullet wound.

And as Walker watched, it healed and closed.

"You can't kill me," Julian hissed. "Nothing can!"

Walker put himself between his daughter, who had awakened and cringed in terror on the bed, and Julian, as screams erupted from the hallway. The sound of shattering glass jerked his attention to the window.

Emma in wolf form, blood staining the white fur of her left ear, growled menacingly with her teeth bared at Julian, the fur at her neck and back standing on end. The rage faded from Julian's face as Emma snapped at him and he took a shaky step backwards. Emma lunged for his leg, forced him back another step. Growling and snarling, she forced him back against what was left of the window, as Walker leapt on the bed to his terrified daughter and pulled her against him.

In his panic, Julian dove out the window to get away from her. Walker expected Emma to go immediately after him, but his breath caught in his throat when she turned back towards him and Melody, teeth bared.

"Emma," Walker tried to make his voice gentle.

Before he knew what was happening she lunged at Melody, her teeth catching his daughter's arm in a quick snapping bite.

"Emma!" Walker cried.

In a flash of gray and white, Emma leapt out the window. He thought he heard a man's screams, but he wasn't sure because Melody's loud wails filled the room.

"My God," Walked gasped at the blood coming from his daughter's little arm. Furiously he yanked the hem of his shirt up, tearing off a generous section of white fabric to use to stop the bleeding. Security guards and deputies swarmed into the room as he wound the fabric around Melody's wound and two nurses rushed up to his side.

"Son of a bitch!" Denny shouted at whatever he saw out the window. "It's a damned wolf!"

Walker scrambled over Melody to jump off the bed just as his friend raised his pistol to fire.

"No!" Walker yelled as knocked his friend's arm away. The pistol fired through the ceiling. In the black night he saw a white shadow, the shadow of a wolf, ceasing its movements and then running away.

From behind, someone cracked him on the head and the white shadow was the last thing he saw.

CHAPTER 6

Walker's eyes flew open. He squinted in the bright morning light from the window next to his bed. What the hell had happened? How long had he been out? Images from the night before flooded his mind, images of Emma and of Julian Beart. And Melody…

He shot up in bed. The quick movement made him wince. Raising a hand to the back of his head, he discovered a sizeable lump and it hurt like hell.

"Sorry about that, buddy."

Denny sat in a chair next to his bed.

"One of my guys didn't know what you were going to do when you hit my arm so he popped you with the butt of his gun." His friend leaned forward to rest his elbows on his knees. "You have to admit it was a pretty crazy scene."

Walker didn't give a shit about that right now. He wanted to see his daughter. And Emma…

"Denny, I—"

Denny held up a hand to stop him. "Everything else can wait, Walker." Were those tears in his friend's eyes? "There is someone waiting to see you."

Jumping up from his chair, Denny marched to the door of the hospital room and walked out. Walker's heart pounded along with his head as watched the doorway. When Denny came back, he was holding the hand of a little girl in a hospital gown. It took Walker a moment to recognize his own child.

Melody beamed at him with a healthy pink face. Gone was the pallor of sickness, the shadows beneath her eyes. Her hair was still gone, but she was walking when she'd been too weak to do so for the last couple of months. A white bandage wrapped around her right forearm, but otherwise his baby looked wonderful. *She looked healthy!*

"Daddy!" Melody squealed as she bounded toward him and climbed easily up on the bed.

Walker caught her face in his hands, stared unbelieving at her shiny blue eyes and her full pink cheeks. He grabbed her hands, too amazed that the needle marks were gone, the bruising had vanished. When he pulled her into his arms, he noticed a big difference. There was energy and tension in her limbs, she didn't feel frail and brittle. *How was it possible?*

"I love you, Daddy," she mumbled against his chest, and he squeezed her all the harder.

He looked up to see Denny wiping at his eyes and a familiar figure standing just behind him. Emma's eyes were shiny with tears. She smiled when noticed he was looking at her.

"I'm going to step out," Denny said, sniffling. He cupped Emma's elbow to take her with him, but Walker stopped him.

"Emma, stay with us."

Denny walked out and closed the door behind him. Emma wrapped her arms about her slim body. She wore a hospital gown, too, and looked exhausted.

"Daddy, do you know Emma?" Melody grinned up at him.

Walker smiled and nodded. "I sure do."

He watched as Emma approached the bed and slowly sat on the edge of the mattress.

"How do you feel?" she asked.

"My head hurts, but I'm okay. How are you?"

Emma nodded. "I'm okay."

"Where's Julian?" He *had* to know.

"He's dead, Walker." Emma's green eyes met his. "What my grandfather said was true. His magic was used against him. His magic is the reason I'm a werewolf. I guess in wolf form I killed him."

Thank God! It was over. And Emma would be in no danger from authorities. They were looking for a wolf.

Walker still wore his own clothes and remembered the necklace had been in his pocket. He reached into that pocket and found it still there. When he pulled it out he immediately noticed the clear bead at its center. The blood was gone.

"Now that he's dead, does that mean you go back to…normal?"

Emma's throat worked as she swallowed. "I don't think so, Walker. If it that was the case, I don't think Melody…"

All at once he understood how it was his child looked as she did, how she was sitting on his lap playing with the broken empty talisman she'd pulled from his fingers.

"You bit her," he remembered.

"Yes."

"So she's a…"

A tear spilled from Emma's eye. "A werewolf? Yes."

Walker felt a tightening in his chest at the stricken look on Emma's face. His daughter would be just like her. While he didn't understand all of the implications of what his daughter had become, one thing was crystal clear. She was *alive.* And looking at her now, if his suspicions were right, she might just live a long time.

That Melody would be a werewolf couldn't be too terrible. That was what Emma was and he loved her.

"I'm so sorry," Emma whispered.

Reaching over, he tipped up her chin with his fingers, peered into her eyes. "Emma, I know you said you don't remember what happens when you change into the wolf. But you saved her. Look at her."

"The blood of the wolf is powerful," her voice was shaky. "But it can't be undone."

"Only one thing really worries me," he threw in.

"Yes?"

"I don't know a damned thing about what this means," he said honestly. "It would be nice to have someone who understood to help me raise her, to help me cope with it."

"I could do that," Emma's voice was low, but he didn't miss the happiness in her eyes.

"I know you could." Walker leaned towards her, took her lips in a gentle kiss. "I want you to. I love you, Emma."

"I love you," Emma said against his lips.

"Awwww," Melody's voice broke into the moment, and Emma smiled at her through her tears while Walker tickled her and made her laugh.

* * *

"Bye, Daddy! Bye, Mommy!"

Melody waved to Walker and Emma as they stood in the doorway of their new house in Searsport. Walker's mother waved, too, as she opened the back door of her car and helped Melody into the child seat. The sun shone brightly off the dark silk of the little girl's hair as she waved back to her.

It's wonderful to see her happy, Emma thought. The doctors had been completely baffled at her miracle recovery from the cancer. A gamut of tests had revealed no trace of it in her little body. Melody was no longer confined to a hospital bed or anywhere for that matter. She'd been through her first few cycles of the moon with Emma and so far things had gone well. The new house had a large wooded area in the back for them to roam when the change came on and Walker was ever vigilant on those nights.

Walker watched Melody and his mother drive away and then smiled at Emma. There was a decidedly predatory quality about that smile.

"Now, we're alone."

Emma's insides melted at the hunger in his eyes as they roamed over her body. Walker closed the front door before backing her against the wall in the foyer, his hands closing over her breasts as claimed her mouth in a passionate kiss. Walker's tongue explored her mouth as the hard length of him pressed against her belly, nudging insistently. His fingers were magic as they slid under her T-shirt and into her bra, teasing her nipples into hard little points.

She gasped when he broke the kiss and slid down her body, sinking onto his heels before her. Emma's fingers sank into his hair as he pulled down her yoga pants and panties. She groaned at the feeling of his warm breath fanning the curls at the top of her thighs. Hooking one of her long legs over his shoulder, he dove for her with his mouth, his fingers spreading her open so his tongue could worry the aching bud that was the center of her pleasure. Her thighs trembled as he devastated her with his mouth, his tongue wild as it teased her clit and darted in and out of her hot ready passage.

Emma was about to come when he stood and hurriedly unfastened his slacks, struggling with his leather belt for a moment before he managed to free his hard, ready cock. Walker pulled one of her legs up to his hip and entered her in the same moment, a single smooth motion, and Emma moaned in pleasure as he filled her, began to drive up into her body as she clenched around him.

Walker lifted her easily so that she could wrap her legs around his waist while he held her pinned to the wall, cupping her ass in his hands.

His thrusts were strong, steady and Emma clutched at his hair, his shirt as the tension came on and the tidal wave of exquisite feeling poised to take her.

"Come for me, Emma," his breath was hot in her ear and it pushed her over the edge as her body convulsed around him and her thighs clamped around his waist. Emma's cried echoed through the foyer as the orgasm rocked her.

He threw his head back as he found his own release, his grip tightening on her as his thrusts slowed. The harsh sound of their breathing filled the small space as they held each other.

Walker kissed her eyelids, her nose. Emma grinned at him. Marriage to Walker had been good for her.

"What?" Walker smiled back at her.

"I'm happy, that's all." Emma kissed him, long and deep. "I love you."

Walker gently let her down and took her in his arms. "I love you, too, Emma. I always will."

Isabella Jordan

Isabella Jordan is the author of several published short stories and articles. By day Isabella is an instructor at a university in her native Virginia. By night she writes erotic tales and fantasies—and eats chocolate! In her spare time she enjoys life. While Isabella enjoys spending quiet time with her family and reading, she also enjoys bungee jumping, hiking, walking in the rain, rock 'n' roll and volunteering at her local women's shelter.

Isabella would love to hear from readers. Please visit her web site at www.isabellajordan.com or write to her at isa@isabellajordan.com.